THE BOOK OF ALL LOVES

Agustín Fernández Mallo was born in La Coruña in 1967, and is a qualified physicist. In 2000 he formulated a self-termed theory of 'post-poetry' which explores connections between art and science. His *Nocilla Trilogy*, published between 2006 and 2009, brought about an important shift in contemporary Spanish writing and paved the way for the birth of a new generation of authors, known as the 'Nocilla Generation'. His essay *Postpoesía: hacia un nuevo paradigma* was shortlisted for the Anagrama Essay Prize in 2009. In 2018 his long essay *Teoría general de la basura (cultura, apropiación, complejidad)* was published by Galaxia Gutenberg, and in the same year his latest novel, *The Things We've Seen*, won the Biblioteca Breve Prize. In 2022, he was awarded the prestigious Eugenio Trías Essay Prize for *La forma de la multitud*. *The Book of All Loves* is his fifth book with Fitzcarraldo Editions.

Thomas Bunstead was born in London in 1982 and lives in Pembrokeshire, west Wales. He has translated leading Spanish-language writers, including Maria Gainza and Enrique Vila-Matas, and won various awards, including an O. Henry Prize and the McGinnis-Ritchie Award in 2022 for his translation of 'The Mad People of Paris' by Rodrigo Blanco Calderón. His own writing has appeared in publications such as the *Brixton Review of Books*, *LitHub* and the *Paris Review*, and he is a Royal Literary Fellow at Swansea University (2022–2024).

'Reading Agustín Fernández Mallo is the closest thing in literature to putting on a VR headset.'
— *La Vanguardia*

'There are certain writers whose work you turn to knowing you'll find extraordinary things there. Borges is one of them, Bolaño another. Agustín Fernández Mallo has become one, too.'
— Chris Power, author of *A Lonely Man*

'The most original and powerful author of his generation in Spain.'
— Mathias Enard, author of *The Annual Banquet of the Gravediggers' Guild*

Praise for *The Things We've Seen*

'*The Things We've Seen* confirms Fernández Mallo as one of the best writers in Spanish, with an absolutely unique style and fictional world.'
— Jorge Carrión, *New York Times in Spanish*

'Charmingly voracious and guided by fanatical precision and wit, Mallo ties the loose threads of the world together into intricate, charismatic knots. This is the expansive, omnivorous sort of novel that threatens to show you every thought you've ever had in a new and effervescent light, along with so many others you couldn't have dreamed.'
— Alexandra Kleeman, author of *Intimations*

'Some great works create worlds from which to look back at ourselves and recalibrate; *The Things We've Seen* takes the world as it is and plays it back through renewed laws of physics. Rarely has a novel left me with such new eyes, an X-ray view of the present.'
— DBC Pierre, author of *Meanwhile in Dopamine City*

'A strange and original sensibility at work – one that combines a deep commitment to the possibilities of art with a gonzo spirit and a complete absence of pretention.'
— Christopher Beha, *Harper's*

'Mallo's imagination never falters. To stay with him means loosening all limitations we might wish to impose on a text. The reward is an audacious adventure.... This is, indeed, a dream of a book.'
— Declan O'Driscoll, *Irish Times*

Praise for the *Nocilla Trilogy*

'A breathtaking work of innovation and heart.'
— Stuart Evers, *Guardian* Best Books of 2015

'By juxtaposing fiction with non-fiction ... the author has created a hybrid genre that mirrors our networked lives, allowing us to inhabit its interstitial spaces. A physician as well as an artist, Fernández Mallo can spot a mermaid's tail in a neutron monitor; estrange theorems into pure poetry.'
— Andrew Gallix, *Independent*

'Bunstead's translation of *Nocilla Dream* is great news not just for those particularly interested in contemporary Spanish literature. It is also simply a wonderful work of avant-gardist fiction – in the line of David Markson, Ben Marcus.'
— Germán Sierra, *Asymptote*

'An encyclopaedia, a survey, a deranged anthropology, *Nocilla Dream* is just the cold-hearted poetics that might see America for what it really is. There is something deeply strange and finally unknowable to this book, in the very best way – a testament to the brilliance of Agustín Fernández Mallo.'
— Ben Marcus, author of *The Flame Alphabet*

Fitzcarraldo Editions

THE BOOK OF ALL LOVES

AGUSTÍN FERNÁNDEZ MALLO

Translated by

THOMAS BUNSTEAD

To Pilar, hic et nunc

'You can look at these true shapes all day
and not see the bird.'
— Anne Carson, 'Audubon'

I.

Looking at the world in silence, and in silence writing what is seen. Writing the silence itself. This is what it is to love the world. (*Silent love*)

Where has it come from, this whole landscape of wounds?
  – he says.
From bodies without passion, which are also landscape.
  – she says.

The first inventory of colours generally agreed to be of any significance was compiled in around 1790, when the botanist Thaddäus Haenke, after numerous expeditions studying the flora of Mexico, Guatemala, New Zealand, the Mariana Islands and the Philippines, felt obliged to catalogue the hundreds of tones until then undetected in the sciences and arts alike. Haenke expanded the known palette from just a few hundred to 2,487 chromatic tones. He completed his map of colours in the same place he ended his days, Cochabamba, Peru, where he tended and studied – study also being a way of tending to things – the garden behind the house he built there. It was said by a number of those who attended his deathbed that what he really wanted to leave behind was not an inventory of colours, but one taking in the gamut of love's tones, its every shade, saturation, texture and glittering. (*Pantone love*)

Our first kiss burned our tongues out completely, and yet still it burns on them.
  – he says.
Paradoxical perfection in bodies that meet.
  – she says.

There is a moment in the experience of love when you start to cut yourself on everything. On the edges of drawers and on the screen of your mobile phone, on your toothbrush and when you're watering a house plant, when you put on your trousers and when you take them off, when you open a book or close a door, when you tie your shoelaces and when you adjust the thermostat on the central heating; even bars of soap and the handrails on buses cut you. Suddenly objects of all kinds want to sharpen their edges on you. (*Blade love*)

The first time I touched you it was like coming home. A home I'd never been in before.
– he says.
Since being with you, I've lost my fear of routine.
– she says.

The lowest manifestation of realism is the extrapolation of statistics about the future. The most naïve manifestation of nostalgia, meanwhile, is the use of those same statistics to make extrapolations about the past. When couples split up, unbeknownst to them, each takes one of these completely opposed approaches. (*Statistical love*)

After the Great Blackout, our hair suddenly turned white. Like the snow on these mountains, which fell one morning and has never gone away.
– she says.
Even polar bear fur isn't white. If you look at each hair closely, one at a time, you'll see that it's transparent.
– he says.

The Vikings, voyaging to the Mediterranean from their frozen northern seas, did not do so hugging the coasts of what we nowadays call Europe. Rather they crossed the continent along the Rhine and other watercourses, skilfully connecting one to the next; navigating fresh water to join two bodies of salt water via the shortest possible route: a kind of cultural geodesic. Along the way they burned towns, animals and the land itself, plundering anything of value – but leaving the flowers on the waysides and, in the cases where they were embroidered, the drapery in people's houses too. It was not that they disliked these things, but that they were invisible to them – the Viking eye untrained for detecting that class of object. Nor did they plunder the beaches themselves when they arrived in what is now Italy; the grains of sand were so smooth, so spherical and gleaming that they did not even see them. What kind of *shortest-line-between-two-points* is this, then, that 'does not see things'? The birds migrating to this continent in the present day also bear in their sexual organs a layer of stamens and ancient minerals that they cannot see and yet scatter as they go. (*Geodesic love*)

When we don't notice the night creeping up on us, it's our vision that's lacking, not the night.
    – she says.
Since the Great Blackout, you've loved me in a different way, you've fed another flame.
    – he says.

The images we see in sleep evolve as we grow older, but then, when we become adults, cease to correspond to the biological body and enter a state of eternal youthfulness: your dream images stop ageing, stop maturing. In old age, and while the march of material degradation continues in the body, the world of sleep and dreams even goes into reverse; at this point, elderly people grow accustomed to the kind of night visions common to the dream life of children. There is no such thing as dreams that belong only to the old, hence their propensity, in waking life, for that strange blend of melancholic yearning for what is lost and an intense hopefulness for the future. And it is not that this asymmetry between the growth of the body and the unfolding of dreams takes place within the passage of time; it is time itself. Nor, when it manifests between two bodies, does love grow any older; love being little more, finally, than a spectre, a constant reverie. And wood is the only material on earth produced by dry seeds, chlorophyll embryos that never grow old. (*Asymmetric love*)

Yesterday, when I picked up that snail which, big and orange like a moving sun, was trying to hide in the grass, and I placed it in the palm of your hand, it slid slowly along and sucked itself onto the tips of your fingers, as though it had grown out of your fingerprints. You watched it and said nothing.
    – he says.
There's a snail sheltering inside my ears too – the only cavity in my body your tongue has yet to explore.
    – she says.

Pueraria lobata is the greatest and fastest colonizing plant on the planet. This perennial vine grows at up to 30 centimetres a day. So predacious is it that in places such as

Florida, Georgia and Alabama it has been classified as a plague. It can swarm forwards over cars and entire homes in a matter of days, burying them under its weight. It scales lampposts, finds its way into sewers, its viridescent network reaching as far as the coast, where still it lives on: it lies around lethargically on grains of sand – tiny pebbles worn down by the ebb and flow of the tides. This began in 1876, when the centennial celebration of the American Declaration of Independence was marked with offerings from a number of countries to this, the greatest country of the New World. France famously gave the Statue of Liberty. Japan's gift was a few samples of *Pueraria lobata*. (*Independence love*)

There's a mausoleum inside our bodies. Our organs have something of both life and death in them, rubble of all we have left behind.
    – she says.
When you allow me to enter you, what I'm trying to do is to bring life to that dead part.
    – he says.

'A person's face does not exist in itself,' Alfred Hitchcock said, 'only when a light shines on it.' An activity that is common but nonetheless just as strange as shining a light on people's faces is the packaging up of things; we package up everything. The internet is only millions of metres of cable that package up the globe. Or take plants, which, left to grow unchecked, would package it up too. Or when people embrace: what is an embrace but the packaging up of the other, giving them a shape unknown to all but you. Or what is choosing one's gender but the packaging up of sex. Meaning there is no need to wrap things up as gifts or send them in the post in order to give them an outline or an identity; light does that for us already. There is no face, once illuminated, that does not fill the beholder's eyes with love. (*Parcel love*)

You and I are nothing.
    – he says.
In a world whose only desire is to devour everything, it's better to be nothing.
    – she says.

What links us to childhood are our Christian names, which stay with us to the end. What links us to childhood is, in other words, language. There is only one thing that an adult cannot do, which is learn to speak. Speech, at the dawn of humanity, was something invented by children, which it still is; every infant's first words mark a new beginning for language. The funny part is that both things – your Christian name, language – come from without, are given to you by others, just as your gender is also given to you. And the years go by, and adult love arrives, which does everything within its power to invert this process, to turn it on its head: when two people are in love they are forever seeking a return to childhood, to create new names, new sexes, to invent a private language, to recast from inside all that is known and create a new roof for them alone; a place to take shelter. This is why the image, present in every culture throughout history, of a couple loving one another under what appears to be a sheet has nothing to do with modesty around nakedness but – in this improvised cave that is theirs and theirs alone – with rebelling against the language imposed in childhood. (*Contra-language love*)

I went to a museum once. Everything there was spectacularly still. It was the most erotic thing I'd ever seen.
   – he says.
A body is also a silent avenue; extreme mute sex.
   – she says.

Falling in love consists of allowing someone to install you inside their head and, once they have you there, trapped forever in their dreams, to do with you as they please; from that moment on you will become a mobile archive inside their body. There is much talk about archives, about the information we register and transmit either through the written word or verbally to those who come after us, but what about that which is forgotten? No archive exists that could ever store all that's forgotten, not because it can never return or be remembered, but because so much is forgotten that the world it occupies is larger than our own by various orders of magnitude. Memory loss, though apparently taking something away from us, also constitutes us. Meaning that when we transmit information, we also transmit all of those forgotten worlds, although in a manner that we are still yet to completely comprehend. This forgetting is me introduced into the heads of others, is my life enclosed in that place, or the part of me accessible only to the person who – in the experience of love – has me inside their head, even though this person (I know) may have forgotten me forever. (*Oblivion love*)

You and I are always airborne, always beating our wings to stop ourselves from crashing to earth.

    – he says.

Do you remember when we went looking for warmth in the perpetual snow?

    – she says, pointing to the snow-capped mountain outside the window.

This science we call economics exists and makes sense only in a world where resources are scarce; if goods and commodities were infinite, there would be no logic to it as a discipline, as it would lose its subject and have nothing to either study or regulate. Our societies have seemingly been constructed on the basis of this congenital scarcity in the world. In western culture, it's already there in the Bible; from the garden that is bountiful without being worked to the disapproval of working for one's daily bread, which will materialize without anyone breaking a sweat. The apparent crisis in the music industry, with its origins in the early 21st century, and the also apparently infinite availability of songs on the Internet, is only the panic experienced in the face of the move from an *economy of (musical) scarcity* – run by a handful of individuals – to an *economy of abundance* – the infinite reproduction of sounds at no apparent cost; a situation in which the economic sciences as currently conceived would cease to have any practical or philosophical meaning. Gender theories have something revealing to offer here: from the masculine/feminine binary, or an economy of sexual identity based on a limited number of genders, to the potentially infinite spectrum of genders in-between that an individual may adopt, a kind of *economy of (gender) abundance* comes about in which learnt social norms lose all validity, giving rise to a panic among those who do not wish to or are unable to give up control of that particular privation. There is a certain structural link between all of this and the incipient field of quantum computing. The foundational property of these future computers is the ability to work not only in binary states, not solely with ones and zeros, but also using everything between the two poles of one and zero, making for potentially infinite possibilities that in turn give rise to worlds and planes of reality not only previously unknown but unimagined, though not therefore impossible. What we could call Gender Abundance Love would therefore be the forerunner, the analogue speartip, as it were, of this other digital abundance towards which computers are heading. (*Gender Abundance Love*)

After the Great Blackout, there were people who asked to be placed inside the pelts of wild animals and buried – animals which, as though sprung from some non-existent nearby forest, had occupied the streets at that time.

– he says.

I helped with those shrouds. We would place the person inside a bag made from the pelts, which we then sewed up. Just before the final stitch, a nameless bird would fly out of the hole in the seam. It was impossible to follow it with your eyes.

– she says.

It sometimes happens that, in trying to get away from someone, you flee so fast and so heedlessly that you end up lost in some unknown place, disoriented, with no idea of what the next step will bring. If it is love we are talking about, we classify these journeys as 'leaving someone without having that someone in mind'. There is no emotional rupture that does not consist of creating such a compass without a map. (*Cut-and-run love*)

Sometimes, when it starts to grow light in the valley and you're still asleep and the early morning sunlight through the window begins to shine on your body, it's like my eyes have never seen you before, like you've come into being simultaneously with the morning. Then I don't know what you're dreaming about, and I start to panic at the possibility I won't recognize you when you wake.
  – she says.
Your face, like water and like uranium, like birds and houseplants, like the sun's corona and like writing, al ready existed before you were born. Your face has been among humans always. That was why I recognized you the moment I saw you.
  – he says.

The fundamental difference between Christianity and Judaism is the greater intellectual dedication required by the latter. Christianity observes certain rituals; Judaism, as well as observing rituals, renders them an object of study. One of the reasons for this difference is that part of Christianity's sacred text, the Bible, was composed of simplified translations of the Torah so that illiterate people could understand, and so propagate, God's Word. Global geopolitics and the attendant conflicts ever since can be boiled down to this ancient and unresolved original separation. As for the way they treat love, both religions manifest the same primitive idea of servitude associated with household pets. (*Pet love*)

I've lost count of the number of years I've spent coming to your body every day to build and destroy the same dream.
   – she says.
But the eternal return doesn't mean the same thing always returning.
   – he says.

Snakes use their tongues, their bifurcate tongues, to smell with. The tips of these tongues detect the concentration of a certain smell to the left or right, prompting the reptile, depending on whether the smell is that of a predator or potential prey, either to alter its course or keep going straight ahead. Something similar happens in the case of pigs and boars with their two nasal holes, which orientate them in survival situations. But this is not so with humans. Our nasal cavities are unable to distinguish between directions; we could have one single orifice rather than two and it would make no difference. The word *amour*, from the Latin *amoris*, is linked etymologically to 'mother'. The ancient Greeks, however, had two different words for love, *eros* and *agape*, which respectively meant carnal love and every kind of affection distinct from sexual satisfaction; a bifurcate kind of love that we lost at some point in history, along with the capacity to orientate ourselves emotionally. (*Bifurcate love*)

God is achromatic now, absolutely neutral in colour, and that's why He doesn't judge me or you but limits Himself to watching the sweat exuded by and then dripping down our bodies. God's only intervention is to make the water inside us symmetrical: if for some reason a drop of sweat appears on my chest, He will make another, identical one appear on yours.

   – she says.

But this divinity knows nothing about what we sweat over inside ourselves, you and I, nothing about our dreams. A nameless bird landed on our windowsill today, the first bird we've seen since the Great Blackout, and it's going to fly through the sky above our heads again and again in the future; which is to say, it will fly through darkness, because it will do so through the absolute night that is the Great Blackout. This means we won't see it, and even if we do, we wouldn't recognize it. It will always be nameless. That which has no name does not exist. Like us: new-made.

   – he says.

The idea of a city empty of humans and abandoned to the elements is a long-standing feature of a wide range of mythologies. Couples build real cities – out of physical matter, out of their affection, out of singular, unrepeatable customs and rituals: a language of their own. The peculiarity of this universe they create is that it isn't destroyed if they split up, but simply enters the condition of *abandoned city*, of a ruin consigned to run its course in some un-specified place. We do not know the exact mutations this city-space undergoes, nor what form it ultimately takes, but what is certain is that, disconnected forever from all that is known, it is an emotional destination that nobody can ever go back to. Not even the people who built it – the former lovers – will get to walk its streets again. The city therefore becomes a literal utopia, the only true utopia there is, such is the disconnectedness but also the violence of its presence. And these things also mean that not even the present-day political dispensation, which as we know yearns for utopias and yet always ends up bringing about dystopias instead, dares go anywhere near it. And it is then, in this abandoned city, that the possibility arises for those of us on the other side to imagine – to idealize – an eternal kind of love: the so-called *romantic love* that enthusiasts for impossible experiences have been cultivating for centuries, with no little success. But romantic love is not the only option. We can look at it in the following way: if it is true that information is neither created nor destroyed, only transformed, it is also possible to think of this world created by the lovers, and now disconnected from our own, as a piece of lost information, a kind of *information-love* that we try in vain to recover on a daily basis. It is a disquieting thing to imagine this city of love, left alone, mutating, taking on new forms, adrift somewhere in the universe, but, at the same time, some gap must exist through which to introduce oneself, if only for brief seconds, to experience in real time the material and emotional information that, with nothing controlling it and as in a distorted mirror of what we once were, still reflects us in its streets. The key question, the one to undo what until now has been an unresolvable knot, would be the following: if in this city of lost love everything is information, what word will it bring? (*Information love*)

When I first met you, long before the Great Blackout, long before we came and inhabited this valley and this house, long before our love grew to such dimensions that we could no longer measure it, a terrible fear came over me of something happening that I once heard about, a story that has been with me since childhood. It's about a man who, any time he speaks, makes his listener grow rapidly older.

– he says.

But that always happens. Naming things, speaking about them, means re-establishing their flow in time, giving them a life that sooner or later will destroy them. Only one thing opposes this kind of entropy: my sex and yours copulating.

– she says.

Lying does not mean not telling the truth. Lying means not telling the truth to someone who has a right to demand it. Even before a corrupt judge or jury, a fundamental legitimate defence sees this principle upheld. Among all relations, from the most mundane to the extraordinary, only in love do we find the exception that confirms this rule: we demand the absolute truth from our beloved even when we have no right to it, an idiosyncrasy that makes love the most vulgar, ordinary and mundane object of all, but also the opposite: the most anomalous and un-mundane. A contradiction in its nature that can only be ascribed to the fact that love – with all the passion and terror it entails – is not another thing *in* the world, not another element in the periodic table of experiences that we go along inventorying, but rather something that corresponds with the warp and weft, the ultimate substrate, of the farthest reaches of our knowledge. Everything is contained in love, and this also includes the place where, in an astonishing and now entirely unimportant blend, true and false find themselves mingled together. (*Substrate love*)

I can't get along with the idea of a book speaking, of the person reading it being able to hear it inside themself. A book is a mute thing, it's the silence of the forest converted into another forest of silence. In all these years in this valley, I haven't read a single book.

– she says.

Yes, you have: the longest and most arcane book ever written, sex between us. Undergrowth that stirs with no wind every sunrise. It speaks inside us.

–he says.

Dust, with all its smells, flavour and texture, is made of the union of excretions and silence. But, inside these new-made motes, there will again be silence, and more of it, a scandalous lack of sound that mysticism seeks to recycle and explain by inventing the presence of a mute, surreptitious god, a divinity that never speaks to us but nonetheless somehow demands that we explain ourselves. Any silence in a film, any white space separating the panels in a comic, any full stop followed by a new sentence on the pages of a novel, the blank spaces on your credit card, and any time two lovers fall silent and look at one another and are suddenly lost for words, it is the terrain of – the living, direct vision of – one moment in the life of this surreptitious, unspeaking god. (*Silence love*)

After so many years lying down together in the same bed, in the same posture, emitting the same bodily sounds, I've come to think that I don't exist, that the repetition makes me dead to you.

– he says.

If only. The dead person never dies again, they're eternal.
– she says.

The fact that teeth and bones are all that remains of us after death is proof that our ultimate identity is mineral. We do not ascend, we are not on some track towards that which the ancients formulated as spiritual; on the contrary, we sink down into the most durable physical matter. A kind of periodic table of elements is what we are; more of the earth even than earth itself. And yet despite this, and paradoxically, we go on being completely ourselves: a DNA analysis of our bones and teeth would not fail to pick out our individual identity. On the night when the world's love of photojournalism killed Diana, Princess of Wales, the boom on the news bulletins eclipsed another event that had more far-reaching consequences: in Algiers, the love of a religious fantasy led to scores of men, women and children being murdered. That night, the princess went to the heaven reserved for martyrs, while the Algerine murderers sank down into a long mineral silence from which their DNA now emerges in the form of so-called radical Islamism. (*Fanatic love*)

When you love truly, as you do, you leave the house and go hunting with all the stealth of that first nameless bird to come and land on our windowsill after the Great Blackout – but also with the strength of a wolf's limbs. Then you come back. You bring your mossy pickings, dry by now, and beetles, too, with only their exoskeletons remaining, and sea salt from I don't know where, and a handful of stones you tore from the hands of the predators that came after you. During your journey those stones have been so eroded that they no longer bear any resemblance to their original shapes; what was all unevenness and rough edges is now smooth pebbles. Not so your body, which comes back honed, whole.

   – he says.

When you love truly, you hunt truly. That's how long the journey takes.

   – she says.

In the past – in the 17th century, say – there was a common motif in anatomical drawings and engravings of a man with no skin standing in a forest clearing, his muscles on show for the benefit of early medical science. Sometimes this man stands with his right arm outstretched and, like somebody holding an empty bag, has the bloody pulp of his own skin, which he has just torn off, in one hand. We know he has torn it off because of the knife in his other hand, blood still dripping from its blade. There is no contemporary explanation for this self-flaying – a person removing their own skin, from head to toe – unless the engravers were trying to tell us that exhibiting one's innards must be done without shame or any thought of modesty, and that neither does the self-flaying imply death, but quite the opposite, converting us into bodies that are useful to science, productive, a fact that must in some way recommend us to some higher, better place. Those 17th-century anatomical engravings would thereby anticipate the fantastical story that is psychoanalysis – if we are considering the exhibition of our intimate selves in private – as well as that other, no less fantastical story of social networks – if we are speaking of the public exhibition of intimacies. *Self-* or *auto-* phenomena are many – *self-adhesive, self-destruction, self-coup, self-combustion, self-hypnosis, self-portrait; automobile, auto-plasty, autograph, auto-ionization*, etc. – and in every case the *self-* or *auto-* is not an end in itself but a tool to address a real future, a space and time both in forward motion. There is only one case of these prefixes turning sterile, serving no purpose whatsoever, and that is when it comes to *self-love*, an impossible emotional equation that asserts the possibility of a love that loves itself. Love is either transitive or it is nothing. (*Non-self-love love*)

I like kissing you with eyes open. Our bodies get so close, it's like your face has only one eye.
– she says.
We're all cyclopes when we kiss.
– he says.

'To man,' says Cirlot, 'things in the world can take one of three shapes: walls, mirrors or windows.' Now, just for fun, we can think of the different kinds of love represented by each of these forms. The wall is familial love: being unable to break through the binds you are born into, that you run up against time and again. The mirror is self-love: that hardly needs explaining. And the window is love of your partner: the glimpsed exterior of a life freely chosen. And if now, again just for fun, we allow a contemporary image to emerge among these archetypes, we should add the word 'porous'. Thus, *porous wall* is familial love in a situation with more than two parents; *porous mirror* would be love for a self of variable identity; and *porous window*, love for more than two partners. But a fourth would also need to be added to Cirlot's basic forms of wall, mirror and window: the *orifice*. The problem here lies in the impossibility of affixing 'porous' to this form; there can be no such thing as a *porous orifice*; its identity can only be absolute. So it goes: the orifice cannot give rise to any kind of modern-day love. There is a reason why in all Indo-European cultures the orifice is associated with all-seeing-ness, but at the same time with that which is most impenetrable, secret and impossible to contemplate in its entirety. The only halfway convincing image today of *orifice love* would therefore be the secret realm of the Deep Web. (*Deep Web love*)

Of all the firewood I've gathered in the years since the Great Blackout, the only piece I haven't put in the pile for burning is this slender branch, which I tied around my neck when it was still green so that it would dry there and I'd never be able to take it off without snapping it. It reminds me of your fingers, clasped together.
   – he says.
That's how you love, that's how you gather the world.
   – she says.

Studies of more than 300 cultures found patterns showing that ecosystems have a direct influence on the cultures that develop in their respective locations; there are only two patterns: the one found in forests – rainy habitats – and the one found in desert habitats. In the cultures that have arisen in the former, such as among nomadic, hunter-gatherer tribes in the Amazon, equatorial Africa and Southeast Asia, there is a tendency towards polytheism, the most physically taxing work is carried out by the men, there is little if any militarism and the sexual customs are unrestricted. In the latter, such as the cultures of the

Bedouins or nomadic tribes in the Sahara or Gobi deserts, monotheism and military structures tend to be the norm, women do the hardest labour, and there is clear religious and social hierarchy, along with strictly regulated rules around sex. We do not have anything from this study on the most extended ecosystem ever seen, that of urban environments, in which the patterns of those 300 cultures blend together to create something unprecedented. We can even think of urban ecosystems as the only ones that give rise to a love of the impossible, to the chimeras people have been dreaming up for centuries; the streets and squares, the cockroaches and starlings, the gardens and the asphalt, the smog and the sewer systems, the lost people and the found, all of which are the incarnation of the most solitary and modest kind of love: the ant that takes itself off to the farthest corner of the deepest layer of asphalt, and there, in peace, like the ancients, gives itself over to death without a sound – neither of love nor of hate. None whatsoever. (*Urban love*)

Look at that billboard. From the time when women's flesh was sold for men's enjoyment.
   – he says.
A show I refuse to repeat.
   – she says.

The one thing that remains unchanged from childhood into old age is a person's gaze, which becomes, thereby, a true identity. The way we use our eyes to look and to express ourselves never changes. Hands are also recognizable throughout a person's life. But there is something else about eyes and hands: they are the parts of the body we move most often; even in sleep, our eyes twitch and our fingers quiver, as though in competition with the unstoppable machinery of our internal organs. Eyes, hands: sentinels which in their constant pumping-out of identity recall a kind of external heart. (*Epidermal love*)

Today, when I went out hunting, I saw a dog – or a mongrel, rather, a wolf-dog sort of thing. It bared its teeth; I showed it my hands. We stayed like that for quite a while, snow statues. Each of us saw our own death in the other's eyes, I think. We feigned battle, then both withdrew.
   – she says.
You have such power, you could hang your clothes on that moonbeam coming in through the window over there.
   – he says.

It is a known fact that in every language the number of words in people's lexicons oscillates between 400 and 5,000, which is the same as saying that there is one group of people that makes use of 400 concepts on a daily basis, and another that makes use of 5,000. Nobody knows why, but it is also a fact that at either end of this spectrum, most words have to do with 'love', which would act upon these two poles of the populace like an elementary, agglutinative mass, a glue for every word spoken. And for everything unspoken too. But, above all, for everything that will never be spoken. (*Poles-apart love*)

Everything – and I mean everything, the tap, wheel,

glasses, tobacco, cups, satellites, music, writing, anything you might wish to name – was tested out in war before being put to civilian use. Every object is the material hangover of some bloody conflict.

    – she says.

I wonder which conflict led to the hangover that is the love invented by our bodies.

    – he says.

In the Spanish language, the word 'omnipresent' – the faculty by which a being or thing is everywhere at once – has no antonym. The dictionary does not specify anything as its opposite. 'Omniabsent' – which we could define as the quality of being nowhere – does not exist. Nor is it a word in any other known language, which relegates the concept from the human sphere entirely. The relationship between omnipresent and omniabsent is therefore different in nature to that between other well-known dualities, such as light/shade, where the one guarantees the existence of the other – shade exists because it is the absence of light – or the duality of good and evil – evil exists because it is the absence of good – and neither can it be compared to the dyad of love/hate – hate being the absence of love. This could lead us to the conclusion that absolute love, if it truly existed, would not necessarily require an opposite; would be an omnipresence that does not admit omniabsence. This object, sought by every civilization as a Holy Grail or as the all-originating primordial ocean, has still not been found. (*Omnipresence love*)

I still haven't reached the extremity of your body.

    – she says.

He says nothing, takes off his clothes and folds them up as though packing for the final journey to the far reaches of the known world, gets into bed and that night dreams of naming the first bird to come and land on the windowsill after the Great Blackout.

If we made the breasts smaller on any Greek statue with a woman's name – such as the Venus de Milo – it would look like a man, such as Apollo. And, vice versa, almost every Hellenic masculine representation would become a woman's body with a little inflation of the chest area. This pseudo-androgynous characteristic of Greek sculptures reappears in Christianity, but joined together in a single figure, that of the angel. Indeed, physically undefined Christian angels can assume different sexes according to their respective missions. The Angel Gabriel we see at the Annunciation is represented as feminine; the same character is present at the Final Judgement, but in a masculine guise. There is a logic to this: all angels are the same angel, an emissary of God's will, and in God everything is Unity, one that, depending on the case, undergoes different metamorphoses. But there is no such thing as God – or at least not yet – meaning that we have been going along creating substitutes for Him. The different religions, whether monotheist or not, for all their declarations to the contrary, are clear examples of doctrines that neither see nor have ever seen any God, and therefore do not work with information that can be retrospectively verified; rather they speak of a non-existent, fictional past, relating events they claim to be true, or invoke a future like somebody who in the middle of a drought repeats the word 'rain' over and over in the hope it will induce the heavens to burst. And then, faced with this lack of real divinities, what happens is that we humans raise ourselves up as Creators. As the following example shows: in the present day, Artificial Intelligence produces entities that are supposedly female or male, symbolically sexed machines that, in the manner of ancient Greek statues, are christened according to purported genitalia – take the case of the domestic robot Alexa. But it wasn't always so; when AI began, in the mid-20th century, it produced machines with no fixed body, assemblages of metal and cables with no predefined symbology, their sex capable of heading in any direction – or none – depending on the use to which the machines were put. We could therefore say that, as far as their bodies went, those machines were angels, the angels of AI. The history of AI is therefore that of a trajectory that inverts the history of bodily representation, having moved from genderless beginnings to the rigid current-day heterosexuality, or, in other words, to the hetero-patriarchalism of the machine. (*Angel of AI love*)

I've discovered a new stream at the top of the valley, it's just beyond the mountain of perpetual snow – I think there are tadpoles, we could go and look at them.
    – he says.
I already saw them a few times, when I was out walking in the early days after the Great Blackout, they were moving about in the little dead hollows of the channels. They wiggled their iridescent tails, restless. Love is blind; from the first to the very last time humans copulate, love is a virus that's forever changing colour, only we never imagine it like this.
    – she says.

Unlike other predators, we humans do not have the kind of teeth that can express an intention to attack. This is why when a stranger approaches, we focus our attention on their hands, on the promise of love or hate contained in these advancing hands, our mandible substitutes. (*Mandible love*)

There's a story that's stuck inside my head, something I heard when I was small and which has been with me ever since: it's about two people of different sexes who converse day and night, for months and years they talk non-stop, and they talk so much and share such a quantity of knowledge, facts and opinions, that they end up swapping sexes without knowing how.

    – she says.

No wonder. I once heard somebody say that the particles which make up the world are all one and the same particle. It takes only a slight twist to turn protons into neutrons, and vice versa.

    – he says.

In geology, 'deep time' is a concept used to refer to chronologies so ancient that it would be unworkable to talk about them in terms of years, and so timescales get subdivided into units like aeons, eras, periods, epochs and ages. Deep time advances so slowly that from the point of view of human scale it could be said to have stopped, to be a kind of time crystallized in physical matter. When someone goes out of your life and, years later, you have the experience of finding things in your home that can be qualified neither as objects – they were never bought – nor as raw material because they are mixtures of many other materials – we call this *love crystallized in matter*. Legitimate vectors of memory, such as a hair. (*Crystallized love*)

Today, coming back from our walk by the river, I trod on a dead grasshopper and said to myself that I couldn't call it a grasshopper any more. In the place where animals go when they die, they lose their names, passing them on to other creatures. As if in this, the body's new home, the dead will christen the living.
   – she says.
I can imagine no greater pleasure than to die in order to give a name to things. I sometimes think that the first bird that landed on our windowsill after the Great Blackout gave us its name so that it could lose it.
   – he says.

The dictionary defines 'immemorial' as 'something so ancient that there is no memory of when it began'. The 'once upon a time' of tales and fables derives from this – a time so distant that all chronology is lost in it, that cannot be dated. This is why time in tales and fables is not properly time; it is outside of measured time. But we can also think of 'immemorial' as something exactly contrary, that which is so near to us, so present and real that it passes from one memory to another without pause, without finding a stopping place or end, and because of that does not stay in anyone's head. In this case 'imme-morial' would be that which in its rapid circulation leaves no trace, which in its continual flow and carrying out of certain objectives is so swift that it will not be *completely used up* by any memory, and may never be remembered.

Love, distant like a children's story but accelerated like the ghost of capitalism, is immemorial in both senses. (*Immemorial love*)

When your body and mine light up in the night like fireflies, the moon darkens. More and more with every passing day.
    – he says.
The sun already did the same. As did artificial light, even earlier on – it gave up on the world of the living with no explanation.
    – she says.

It is animals, not us, who live in the prison-house of language, because they are not able to leave and stand outside it and think about it. This is only because it is impossible for them to access the ideas that surround words. A dog never crosses a road, because it does not know what a road is. This, among other things, is why dogs get run over. It isn't that the dog fails to look both ways before crossing, it's that it does not possess the idea of a road. Its gaze is another gaze, its crossing is another crossing. Hence the fact that an animal cannot give or receive love either. It's not that it doesn't love, it's that its love is *other*. (*Language love*)

In all these years I have found infinite happiness in your cavities. As if they too were infinite.
    – he says.
They're finite, though they have an end. If not, every-thing we pour into them would be lost, you and I would

have no memory of each other.
  – she says.

A test tube, a common feature of research laboratories
and clinical-trial settings, is, if we stop to think about it,
incorrectly named. To be a 'tube' it would need to have
openings at both ends; really it should be a 'test receptacle'.
Moreover, the word 'test' does not entirely match what it
does; the test tube serves to try out hypotheses, but also to
demonstrate them, so this part of the name isn't entirely
satisfactory either. If we now consider its shape, we will
see that its length and diameter conform to certain strict
measurements, shared by test tubes the world over; every
single test tube could be said to be the same test tube. For
example, though it is well known that everything in the
United States is larger than in Europe, all objects there
being larger by a scale factor of approximately 1.1, or that
the opposite is true in Japan, things there being smaller
than in Europe by a scale factor of 0.9 – despite this – test
tubes are the same in Europe, the United States, Japan,
Africa and Oceania. Just as they will be even on Mars if
the red planet should ever be colonized. But the shape
of the test tube has more to tell us still: we know that all
cultures have come up with their own ideal norms when
it comes to the human body, something founded as much
in mathematical ideas as in symbolic images. The ancient Egyptians took the fist as their corporeal reference
point; the ideal human body for them was 18 fists tall.
The ancient Greek norm took as its reference the 7 heads
proposed by Polykleitos, which Michelangelo increased
to 7½ and Leonardo to 8. The Christo-Roman imaginary
put forward a very different norm, symbolically related
to evolving representations of Christ's body, which never

matched the rule imposed by the Greeks, meaning that in those centuries Christ always appeared slightly deformed or misshapen. Nor did the norms in the ancient cultures of India, New Guinea or what today is Mexico – all of them fundamentally symbolic – bear any relation with our own. In the 20th century, the most well-known scale of proportions in the West was proposed by Le Corbusier, which he called Modulor, and which is used in the design of living spaces and domestic furniture. Be that as it may, what interests us here, the real discovery, comes when we pause to note that the proportions of a test tube's height and diameter are the same as those of our arms and legs; the relationship between the height/diameter of the average human leg is the same as the relationship between the height/diameter of a test tube. And the relationship between the height/diameter of the average human arm is also the same as that between the height/diameter of a test tube. The test tube is not only identical in every laboratory and culture on the planet but in its proportionality is identical to the proportionality seen in every human body, which makes it the overlooked and perhaps secret norm of the contemporary human. As a corollary, it is clear that the body, our body – and this includes all the affection and love that our flesh gives off – has its natural extension today in the praxis of the laboratory. (*Test-tube love*)

I also don't know what gets in our way when we pass by the ruins of the houses that stayed standing after the Great Blackout. I suspect it's the souls of the people who inhabited them, who perished in the doorways as they tried to flee in terror.

    – he says.

Until we have loved one another inside all these dwellings,

our love will be incomplete. The death of the human race is a puzzle we must solve with our bodies.

– she says.

VENICE (1)

Month of June, first floor of a palazzo whose foundations stand below the waterline of Venice's Misericordia Canal. There is a room, and a high window with views across the domes of St Mark's Basilica and across a sea that will shift in colour throughout the day. There is also a woman – a writer – who, were she to look up, would be able to see all of this, but keeps her eyes down instead, tapping at the keys of a typewriter. Her typing produces slight movements in a small snow globe containing a miniature version of Venice to her right on the desk, raising a layer of snow up inside the globe, where it swirls before falling across the plastic city, and the writer goes on typing, and on, while outside, in the real Venice, the Venice of tourists and water and stone, the June humidity ushers in an early summer storm. Now, as the sequence she is working on grows in intensity, the table turns quivering fingerboard and the snow rises in the globe, and again it rises, once more hitting the tiny glass vault and falling on empty palazzos and waterless canals. The books and papers strewn across the desk, all of them on one single subject – love – receive these blows without so much as a flinch. Inside the globe, a snowflake has just landed on St Mark's Square, filling it completely; at the same time, outside, in the city of tourists and water and stone, a flash of June lightning illuminates the skyline of palazzo silhouettes. And now she feels the ache in her fingers – these old typewriters so unforgiving – a couple of broken fingernails she's forever thinking of cutting and forever failing to. She stops, as does the vibrating of the desk. Nothing moves in the sky of the globe, its streets have become white sheets, the glass dome inviolate, and the thought that comes to her is, When it snows, where do birds go?

When it snows, where do birds go? the writer again says to herself. Her husband is asleep in the next room, he's been sleeping for days now, and she gets up, moves away from the desk, looks down at the street below through the high, first-floor window of this palazzo, a holiday let they managed to rent for next to nothing and where they have spent the last six months; the estate agency has had no problem extending their stay for as long as the couple wish. We say the couple have spent the last six months in the palazzo, but this is not entirely accurate. We find ourselves in June and, though they did arrive in January from their home in Montevideo, after the initially planned fortnight of tourism in La Serenissima, and for reasons never entirely explained, the husband announced that he was going to stay on, that he had no intention of leaving Venice, meaning she had to return to Uruguay alone. Now, six months on, she has come back for him, has come back because she does not understand what he could possibly be doing in Venice all on his own, and they have spoken – or, rather, they have not, silent meetings that say more than an entire alphabet. And so she has sat down and begun to type, possibly to impose some order on the silence that like armour plating has descended between them; imposing order on a typewriter's jumbled alphabet. Through the wall she hears her husband shifting in the bed. The mattress and sheets rustle, only to abruptly fall quiet again.

44

A flash of lighting, still far away in the distance, splits the study in half; she stops typing. Back at the window again, she stands and watches as a gondola disappears around a bend, observing how little the gondolier must move his body to swing the vessel completely about, and she remembers being in Montevideo airport at 2.30 a.m. just a few days ago, about to take the flight that would bring her back to Venice to be reunited with her husband. She remembers the deserted building and sees herself moving forward through Arrivals, alone and completely untethered. Not many people know that there is a *first instant* to every airport, a number of seconds, sometimes as long as a few minutes, in which not a single passenger is present and the airport installations as a whole cease to carry out their stated function, become something else. After clearing security, she went and bought a bottle of water from a vending machine before exploring Zone C, stopping and looking in at the shuttered shops and the window displays of souvenirs, and thinking how these plastic and metal miniatures summarized not only a country but an entire state of mind. We are all souvenirs of an idea, of a perversion, of a nation, of a person, of whatever it might be; we do not possess souvenirs, they possess us. And although it was beyond her to understand why a souvenir of an Italian city was being sold in Montevideo International Airport, in the only open shop she bought a snowglobe containing the city of Venice; suddenly the idea of giving it to her husband appealed. She said as much to the man working in the shop, who, carefully wrapping up the globe for her, said, 'There's a reason the airport's called the International – you can find everything here. And anyway, is there anything in the world nowadays that isn't international?' The writer remembers wandering the airport those few days before, and now, in the Venetian palazzo, goes back to her desk and starts typing again, about the only subject of interest to her, love. A sudden flash from the east, from the older part of the city, again splits the study in two. The summer storm is growing nearer. By the time the sound of the thunder reaches her, she will already have written a further 200 words, more, the snowglobe will have bobbed up and down on the desk and snow will have fallen a corresponding number of times on the miniature St Mark's Square.

Montevideo Airport, 2.30 a.m.: the only passenger in the departure lounge, a solitude that conferred a cathedral air on the ceilings, a solitude in which she thought ahead to her arrival in Venice, the palazzo, leaving her suitcase by the door, a long, passionate kiss, then him unwrapping the gift and his look of surprise at the snowglobe of Venice, brought to Venice from so far away. But this would be the following day; for now, the other passengers soon started to arrive at the boarding gate. A man came and sat down opposite her; tall and slim with a silver head of hair, he must have been in his eighties. His face seemed familiar. It took her a few minutes to remember that she had seen him six months earlier, when first in Venice; it was strange to see him now, all this way from the Italian city. She and her husband had passed him several times in the street and been struck by his movie-ambassador get-up: the blue double-breasted blazer, the gold buttons and burgundy tie. The man crossed his legs just as they exchanged glances, and he soon got up, went over to the drinks machine and bought himself a small bottle of water, sidestepping a group of passengers on his way back to his seat, drinking the water practically in two swigs, keeping the empty bottle in his hands, seeming almost to caress it as he fixed his gaze on some indeterminate point on the departure-lounge wall, when, as he went on gazing, he looked more like a Berber to her than an ambassador.

The writer knows about Berbers and their customs because in her twenties, on a trip to the Atlas Mountains in Morocco, she had a guide who was a member of this tea-addicted indigenous people – addicts to visions of the other world, too. She remembered how no task had seemed beyond this man. If she needed water, he would stop the car, disappear off beyond a ditch and come back with the exact quantity of liquid required; if it started to grow dark and she was cold, he would pull up just where dry grass could be gathered as kindling, and they would then sit beside a small campfire, and he would start boiling some exceptionally clear water to make tea. She was in that part of Africa because she wanted to traverse the former weapon- and gem-smuggling route – stretching over vast distances and by then all but vanished – between Algiers and the Moroccan portion of the Atlas Mountains; the aim, to research and gather information about people's diets and eating customs, in particular the recipes once used by the men and women who had roamed those lawless routes in centuries gone by; a clandestine path must, she wanted to prove, in some way correspond with meals that were also clandestine, existing beyond the margins of known menus and diets. In her memory, that man of the Atlas Mountains looked down into the dregs of his tea for a few moments and suddenly began to talk about his favourite animals to hunt, which were leopards, because leopard blood was the only kind that was good to drink as well as to eat fried, fried in the leopard's own fat, 'Discounting pigs and seals,' he said, 'it must be the only animal with which such tautologies are possible, but my religion prevents me from eating pork, and there are no seals in the desert. So, leopards are like the pigs of my culture.' She said nothing, made a note. To one side, the desert in the last of the daylight, which fades so mysteriously; to the other, the Atlas Mountains, which burst up out of the plain to soar some 4,000 metres to the perennially snow-capped Mount Toubkal. And in her memory the man stoked the fire and took a sip of his tea before pointing up at the summit: 'What's up there that there's none of down here?' he said. In response to her silence and the shrug of her shoulders, the Berber went on: 'Kilimanjaro is a snow-covered mountain 19,710 feet high, and is said to be the highest mountain in Africa. Its western summit is called the Masai "Ngáje Ngái", the House of God. Close to the western summit there is the dried and frozen carcass of a leopard. No one has explained what the leopard was seeking at that altitude,' at which he paused to share some of his tea with her, before continuing: 'That's the opening of "The Snows of Kilimanjaro", the short story by Ernest Hemingway, which you, being a writer, surely recognize, but you ought to know that the leopard Hemingway talks about, the real leopard, a leopard that the writer never saw, is not on Kilimanjaro but up there, on Toubkal,' he gestured at the mountains again, 'and, what's more, it isn't a male but a female leopard, a leopardess called Alexandra in the local traditions, originally a Greek name, brought to these lands by the Romans. It means "Protector of Humanity". The bones of that female cat, she who protects us, are up on that peak. All of us here have seen her, the ice up there is particularly transparent, as transparent as the water of the River Ourika and as the ice cubes they were selling at the last petrol station we passed yesterday, at the last crossroads, 100 kilometres north – ice cubes made with water from that very river. You get foreigners coming here just to see the purity of the ice cubes at that petrol station; you can look through them and there's absolutely no distortion to what you see on the other side, prisms so perfectly transparent that you almost don't see them, like they're imaginary. People try to take the ice cubes with them, as proof of the most crystalline water there has ever been, but they melt along the way. They mix them in with their soft drinks, with tea or simply with other water in their water bottles, and when they get home, drink them like holy water. And all this water comes from the slow melting of the ice cap at the summit of Toubkal, where it lays three metres thick, covering the body of our protectress, Alexandra, ice so crystal clear that, if you look in the big cat's eyes, you see the last vision she experienced, the vision of death itself. Yes, the face of death could be said to be lying up there.' Then the Berber placed his tea down on the ground beside his goatskin backpack, followed by something the writer did not initially understand: he took a photograph out of the inside pocket of his jacket, a picture of himself silhouetted in front of a mud-and-straw settlement, and threw it in the fire, simply threw it in, in a boomerang motion, but one from which there would be no coming back. In less than a minute the glossy paper had been reduced to a thin layer of carbon, during which time the writer watched the slow tide of fire climbing up the body of a man in the picture, eventually invading his face completely. The Berber, also saying nothing, observed this combustion of his own body. The writer felt that an ancient secret was latent in such a silence, though the nature of it evaded her. They stayed like that for some minutes, until he got up, said he was tired and for the first time asked if he could spend the night in the car they had hired several days before. She said it was fine by her, deciding to sleep under the stars for the first time, next to the fire. She was a small woman and did not need a great blaze to keep warm. When the sun woke her the next morning it was still cold. As she had learned from the Berber in their days together, she gathered some dry grass and made a small fire – big enough to heat the water for breakfast. Coaxing it to life, she saw that the burnt remnants of the photograph were still visible in the previous day's embers. Then she went over to the car with its tinted windows. It took her a few seconds to see that the man was not inside. She looked down: there were two sets of footprints beginning from the car door; one went north, into the desert, and the other south, towards the summit of Mount Toubkal. The writer moved back a few steps to get a better view: in both directions, the same size sandals and the same shaped soles. She did not, could not understand. In her mind's eye she saw the photograph they had put in the fire the previous night. It was as though reducing someone's image to ash meant, rather than destroying it, multiplying it by two.

The writer continues typing, her husband asleep in the next room, the snowglobe jolting up and down on the desk and snow falling on the miniature Venice, while outside, in the city of water, tourists and stone, the summer storm continues to approach, and she sees lightning once more, still far off, and goes on casting her mind back to her flight from Montevideo to Venice a few days before. She remembers she had been in luck when she boarded: her row was unoccupied, two seats entirely to herself. She was wearing a white blouse with black pearly buttons; she had found it with her husband six months before, in January, during their first stay in Venice. Someone had dropped it in the street, and she had instantly been drawn to it; the material had a comforting effect on her heart, it made the beating in her chest seem softer, less staccato. The aeroplane climbed higher, leaving behind it the Río de la Plata delta, grey and turbid as ever, and the writer soon saw that skipping breakfast had been a sensible thing to do; until they reached altitude, the turbulence was terrible. She heard someone at the back throwing up, turned around to look. She was surprised to see only one other passenger in the tail section with her, but also that it was the man she had seen in the departure lounge, the one who looked like an ambassador – who in turn looked like a Berber man who many years before she had seen split into two people and disappear into the Atlas Mountains. They caught one another's eye, she immediately turned to look forward again. Her husband came to mind, she remembered him, over the phone from Venice to Montevideo, saying he wasn't going to meet her at the airport, and to take the vaporetto taxi, and her feeling wrongfooted by this; despite the magnetism of the voices, and due to some effect that remains unexplained to this day, things sound much further away and more unreal over the phone than in writing. The turbulence subsided, and with it the man's vomiting. She looked out of the window. The sun was shining; above the cloud layer the sun always shines. The tip of the wing gleamed, it looked slightly curved to her, and she found something troubling in this. They soon turned off the lights.

The passengers slept, they slept like the dead, she too closed her eyes but did not fall asleep, recalling instead the first trip to Venice, six months earlier, in January, with her husband. The moment they landed, they had immediately set about the things they wanted to do. The estate agent had given them the keys to the palazzo's first-floor apartment, before reeling off some suggestions on the city in general and about the Misericordia Canal area, not that many but enough for the fortnight they were due to stay, and before he left briefly advised them that there was something missing from the furnishings, but the landlord had given it to him, and that he would have a courier bring it later on. It was not only the first time they had been in Venice as a couple but also the first time they had been somewhere snowy together, a double novelty that felt overwhelming at first. They saw shop displays with pieces of jewellery selling for more than €20,000, and birds flying impassively through the snow clouds. She remembered that they had decided to waste no time in visiting one of the areas they were most excited to see, the gardens where the famous Art Biennale was traditionally held; nothing was going on there at the time, but for them it was enough to see all the different countries' pavilions from the outside and to stroll in the woods around them. Snow began to fall, soon turning to heavy rain; very grudgingly they broke off their visit. In the afternoon they ate spinach and ham focaccias in the rain. They passed a taxidermists', where a neatly arranged collection of squirrels, hares and seagulls in the window display seemed to be trying to catch their eye. They peered in at the window. Inside, all the way at the back, various men and women were working on what appeared to be deer, big cats and other large animals. He became entranced by the eyes of one of them, a leopard; half-visible behind the counter, the taxidermists had not finished working on it. She remembered saying then that the key moment in taxidermy is when the artisan picks out from her or his catalogue the eyes with pupils whose exact colour and shape 'will give the animal the same depth as it had in life, and so extract it from death'. The sun had come out after that, the sun always comes out, and on his insistence they had gone around the up-market clothes shops in the vicinity of the Rialto Bridge. She, naturally elegant but at the same time opposed to the prestige associated with big labels, waited for him outside; she stood watching the women and men on the terraces drinking sophisticated mineral water under the shelter of outdoor gas heaters; the towering flames seemed to spring from the pavement itself. The rest of the excursion to those lavish shops was lost to her, but she did recall, when they later became disoriented in the winding streets of the same quarter, that it was then they had seen the man who looked like an ambassador for the first time; sitting on a terrace, he was drinking a glass of water. It was too fleeting to be qualified as a vision, but in the few seconds it lasted, she felt the full force of a memory, an entire memory, that she had thought forgotten: in her twenties, and after years of not setting foot in a church, she had been obliged to go to the funeral of a close girlfriend, and arrived at the last possible moment, as non-believers tend to. The church was full, but she managed to get a seat in a corner at the back, beside a loudspeaker that hung down from a pillar. The PA system was not on; the excellent acoustics in the central nave meant there was no need for the priest to shout. And it was almost at the end when it happened. While one of the family members was again evoking the life and miracles of the dead girl, she had begun to hear breathing coming through the speaker next to her, a few centimetres from her ear. She quickly realized that the sound, rather than magnetic interference, was that of an actual mouth inhaling and exhaling, like when you wake in the night and cannot get back to sleep, and lie there listening to the breathing of the person beside you.

After a couple of minutes, the sound simply stopped. The priest invited people to go and take Communion, and she, on an impulse, went and joined the queue to the altar. Although it was only the once in her life, she had felt the absolute necessity of experiencing mortal sin.

On another day during that first stay in Venice, on a street near the palazzo, he noticed a statue on the façade of a building that was missing both eyes, he said nothing, but found such vandalism incomprehensible; to take a statue's eyes is equivalent to taking the eyes from all the world's living statues: the humans. After that they had gone in and out of a multitude of cafés in search of some coffee that was not extortionate. It was raining, but the rain failed to melt the snow; on the contrary, the cold was such that the raindrops solidified into tiny spheres on impact, giving the frozen canals and the streets the look of a star-strewn sky; the couple imagined how many constellations they could create by joining them all together, before going on walking again, mixing the snow and ice back together. And it was when they turned the corner onto another street, relatively deserted and sunless, that they saw the blouse on the ground. At first its whiteness made it almost indistinguishable from the snow, but then they saw the pearly black buttons – neither was its fabric snow nor of course were the buttons dirty drops of ice. Completely spread out, it looked as though it had been dropped there by the city itself. She remembered her husband asking if it was a blouse or a man's shirt, and her saying not to be so old-fashioned. They looked at it in silence for several seconds before going over, only, when they did, to both recoil: under the material, at chest level, there was a raised lump of some sort that was expanding and contracting. 'Like a heart,' she said. 'It must be a little fish from the canals – they've overflowed in certain places in the city.' He thought this impossible, that it was probably a small bird fallen from a nest in a tree, but she pointed out that there were no trees in Venice. The lump then suddenly started to move, darting up to the right shoulder where, more slowly now, it turned and went down along the sleeve. A rat's snout emerged from the end of the sleeve. On coming into contact with the light, the creature seemed to take fright, and it scurried back underneath the blouse as quickly as it could, curling up again at the heart of it. It was still beating as they turned and walked away.

They returned to the palazzo that night to find a delivery man in the doorway, 'I've brought this package, it's from the estate agency for the people on the first floor, is that you? Sign here.' As they went to go inside, he joked that the staircase, which was a very steep near-spiral, looked like a throat that was about to swallow everything. They went through to the living room and opened the package, which was no bigger than a shoebox. It took them some minutes to understand that the cylindrical, golden object before them was an Alexa, the personal assistant. The note read: 'On behalf of the landlord we are sending you this device, to be of assistance during your stay in Venice. Regards.' The small device spontaneously connected to the Wi-Fi network, and a blue ring of light appeared at its heart. Taken aback by this round, pulsing thing, for a few seconds they simply stood there. 'It looks like a heart,' he said. 'More like an eye,' she said. In bed that night, the darkness broken only by the blinking of the blue ring of light, which reached them from the living room, she, speaking very quietly so as not to be heard by Alexa, whispered in his ear: 'Where does Alexa's name come from?' After a few moments' thought, and also speaking very quietly, he said: 'It's an abbreviation of Alexandra, a Greek name that means protectress of humanity.' She was about to say something else, but understood that his slow response had been because he was falling asleep – she knew he didn't want for knowledge in dead languages – as demonstrated by the successive snores that followed. She curled up into a ball under the sheets and thought what Alexa would be making of these shapeless sounds issuing from some place in her husband's throat. The next day, as soon as they were woken by the sunlight breaking through the blinds, they shared an unusually long, deep kiss, and, as though he had spent the night considering her question, the first thing he said when they broke off was, 'I should also say that the great Greek poem recounting the end of the world is called *Alexandra*, Lycophron wrote it and it gives a complete account of Greece's history, from Troy to the Roman conquest, an entire civilization hurtling towards extinction.'

On another day, on the advice of an altar boy who they had spoken to by chance in the Church of Mary Magdalene, after happening to find him in the sacristy listening to vinyl records, they went to a second-hand record shop nearby on the Santa Catarina canal. It had the yellowing air of an antique shop, broken up only by the black of one record or another being removed from its sleeve, a blackness that to her seemed as imperturbable a carbon star. A feature of the shop was that it had a recording studio; anybody could go along and record anything they wanted – a song as a keepsake, a speech sending birthday wishes to a grandmother, whatever it might be – and within a few minutes, having parted with a considerable sum of money, leave the shop with a 33rpm single-press

vinyl under their arm. The standard recording proce-
dure was used, the same as had been in operation since
the early years of the phonographic industry, which is
simple and has barely altered over time: you step inside
the booth, where the vibrations of your voice and any
instruments are sent through the microphones to a turntable very similar to the kind on a normal record player,
but bearing a vinyl record that is totally smooth, virgin,
and with a thicker needle, which vibrates with the elec-
trically delivered sound. This vibration literally gouges
the vinyl in real time, opening up the micro-groove, the
sonic footprint we then see on the vinyls we listen to
later on. Minutes earlier, on the way to the shop, he had
already made a comment that related to all of this: 'I find
it strange that the trees in cities don't leave grooves and
micro-grooves on the buildings' façades,' he said. 'When
you see them moving in the wind, it's as though they're
going to record their particular tree sound on the walls
of the houses, but they never do, and neither does the
grass in people's gardens, which just keeps to its appoint-
ed sections.' In the shop, they went their own ways. She
browsed in a section containing hard-to-find American
No Wave from the late seventies, becoming so absorbed
that she lost track of time, until he came over to say he was
bored with the classical section now, where he had been
listening to some early Chopin recordings; in fact, he had
bought one, a collector's item, as he showed her, holding
up the plastic bag. On the way back, snow began to fall,
and they tried to go through St Mark's Square but found
it had been cordoned off: although nobody could explain
why, it appeared that a great bubble of total soundlessness
had installed itself in that part of the city. 'When you enter
the square, all sound disappears,' said the policeman at
the cordon, who was wearing a camouflage face mask, 'it's

as though your ears have been emptied out, it's never happened anywhere before, no one knows of anything like it – plus, as well as this total lack of sound, anyone who goes out into the middle gets an intense migraine.' Annoyed by this, they had to make do with the view of the deserted square, along with the basilica, its ornamented façade still and white like a mountain of perpetual snow. They set off for the palazzo. At the last bridge along the way, he said: 'Since we left the record shop, there's something I haven't been able to get out of my head.' 'What's that?' she said. 'I've realized that all things have grooves in them. The asphalt we walk on and the clothes we wear, the stones in the forests and the roofs of houses, the designs on the leather of people's shoes and dogs with their muzzles, they all have their own grooves and micro-grooves... I think everything must have its own sound and every object its own particular music. True, we don't know what needle would be capable of extracting this soundtrack from the world, nor what it would sound like, but logic surely dictates that all these melodies *should* exist, don't you think?' She nodded, watching a group of seagulls flying low over the wake of boats and gondolas, the choppy, ceaseless water gradually eroding the buildings' foundations. A few minutes later, back at the palazzo, the leopard came to mind – the stuffed specimen that had had such a hypnotizing effect on her husband a few days earlier, and as she hung up her coat in the entranceway, she said: 'Hey, what's "leopard" in Latin?', to which he immediately responded: '*Leopardus*, which is *leo*, or lion, and *pardus*, or panther, joined together. The ancients thought it was a bastard animal, a weird vestige, the result of an unnatural union between a panther and a lion.' They had a supper of rice with strips of beef, cooked by her, a meal she often made, this time adding some shredded, flash-fried cabbage. When she cut up the vegetable, with a single, sagittal slice, she spent several seconds observing the intricate forms of its leaves, each labyrinthinely enclosing the next. These cabbage leaves seemed like a fossil to her, a landscape being seen for the very first time.

In another of their walks during that first stay together in Venice, they passed a blind man; the uniform movement of his legs was the only physical clue to his condition. She said: 'I've seen a lot of blind people these last couple of days.' Barely minutes later, on their way to a restaurant, they walked past a woman with milky-white eyes; 'White like the snow we're walking on,' said the writer. Over the days that followed, and perhaps because it had been pointed out to him, he too noticed blind people frequently crossing their path. That night, while he was watching television in the living room, she looked up from her book and said that the city was being taken over by the blind, that she was sure of it, and not the sort of blind people one used to get, but rather those who had lost their vision suddenly, so that they didn't have time to access the special sensitivity that develops when one is blind from birth. This brought to mind an old story, the name of which escaped her, which she had read in a book by a French author, Boris Vian, nowadays virtually forgotten: 'It's about a city where, without the meteorologists having seen it coming, a dense fog moves in one day, so dense that the people in the city can see no more than a couple of centimetres ahead of them. At first, frightened both of the heavens and of their fellow humans, they go and huddle in the farthest, most hidden corners in their homes. It isn't long, though, before they realize how little sense this makes: they're no more hidden at the bottom of a deep hole that they are out in the middle of the widest of open spaces. The entire city is a continuous mass of milk-coloured cloud, which, in time, the people not only get used to, but causes them to lose all inhibitions. They start going out naked in the streets, helping themselves to whatever they want from shops without paying, they fornicate with the first person they bump into, that sort of thing. The happiness they experience is like the kind associated with the god Pan. Then one day, just like that, the fog clears. An unbearable feeling of shame takes hold of the people, followed by embarrassment at all the acts they've committed, and again they hide away, thinking never to come out; some even take their own lives. The situation becomes very alarming, and a citizen council is urgently convened. After days of heated debate, a swift return to that happy state of shared blindness is proposed: they decree that the entire populace must have their eyes put out. Boris Vian's story ends there... Fine, so at this point, it seems to me beyond question that the city of Venice has begun a slow process that's leading towards this kind of blindness... By the way, what's "blind" in Latin?' '*Caecus*,' he said, 'it's *caecus*.'

On a day during that first stay in Venice when it was too cold and windy to venture out, they decided to spend the morning listening to the Chopin record on the palazzo's excellent sound system and cooking using ingredients and condiments beyond their usual round, raw materials they knew about from books on Marco Polo's explorations and from the *Meals of the World* publications she had collected as a child and could almost claim to have memorized. While she picked out ingredients and he, sitting on the sofa, watched the blue pulsing coming from the small golden cylinder that was Alexa, the crazy idea came to him that the little machine was copying everything, that its mission was to register every single sound in the palazzo, every conversation and every noise coming in from outside too, but not to establish the patterns of people's tastes and thereby enable the powers that be to control us emotionally, but quite the opposite, in order to forget us – with all this data in hand, to construct a parallel world elsewhere, a new version of nature that would leave humanity behind once and for all. An idea he found far more unsettling than the one about control. As if, rather than being a fount of all known information, Alexa were the creator of previously unimagined combinations of realities, a primitive quantum computer. They ended up making a simple rice dish with strips of beef; she knew by heart the ingredients of the dishes in *Meals of the World*, yes, but said she suddenly had no idea how to use them; inexplicably, when it came to it, her hands went into knots, wouldn't move.

On another day, during a late morning breakfast – her putting so much jam on her toast that it was like she wanted to drown it forever – he told her about his dream the night before: 'I dreamed that the two of us were sleeping, here, in the bedroom, and that I was woken up by some noises. Since I'm not that familiar with this building, I thought it was the normal kind of creaking you get in old places, but it quickly turned into a sort of rattling in the front-door lock; someone was clearly trying to open the door. In the dream, I woke you up and the two of us lay there, completely still, frozen like two mice in a snow hole, transfixed as the noises became clearer, until we heard the door hinges. You jumped out of bed, I followed you and we walked hand in hand to the entranceway where, next to the big living-room table, there were three men in jumpsuits – in the darkness they looked blue – and they put down some cardboard boxes which were very big but, from the way they handled them, seemed extremely light, empty. They looked at us, and after a brief silence said they'd been coming to the house for years, looking for something, though they themselves didn't know what. Then they just left – they closed the door but left the boxes. You and I, we didn't so much as touch the boxes, but just went back to bed.'

On another of those days they agreed to go out on a long excursion by gondola, something they had been wanting to do: to see the city not only from the water but at water level gives an idea of just how majestic the palaces and homes are; even the humblest of boat shacks grows immeasurably. Entranced by the gusts of wind and the water splashing up in their faces, they sailed around in silence; everything in this world seemed new-made. Looking at the gondola seat, the red velvet upholstery, he said: 'Sometimes, when it's night and you're asleep, boats go by very slowly underneath the window, and I hear the slapping of the water on the canal, which never stops, I've been doing something that makes no sense: I get up and sit on the living-room sofa in the darkness, waiting for the men who, like in my dream, bring cardboard boxes in the middle of the night. I know it's stupid, thinking a dream might actually happen, but still I do it. Do you think a dream can become reality?' She did not answer, closed her eyes so she could focus on the weak rays of sunshine bathing her face. After the gondola ride, they consulted the map and saw that there was a shortcut back to the palazzo, and instantly decided to take it; it was growing dark and he said he was freezing cold. On one of the first streets they went down, they realized they had gone that way before: there in the distance was the white blouse with the black pearly buttons; it was still lying on the ground. There were no animals pulsing in its heart now. The ice had melted and the material, hard as a skeleton, lay directly on the stone. She was about to mention a leopard on an African mountain also waiting for the ice that covered it to thaw, but instead just picked up the blouse and put it in her bag, and they carried on. They arrived back at the palazzo, took the stairs, which looked more like a throat to them than ever, and as soon as they were inside she went to the bathroom, washed the blouse by hand, hung it out over the bath. She wore it the next day. During the rest of the trip, the only time she took it off was to wash it.

On another day they stopped at a restaurant next to the Ponte dell'Accademia with good views out over a jetty. The menu claimed they had the cheesiest pizza in Venice. He ordered a glass of white wine; she had water. He took a slice of pizza in his hands; to her the long strands of melting cheese looked like lightning bolts. She said, 'What's "lightning" in Latin?' '*Fulgur*,' he said once he had managed to deal with all the cheese, 'it's *fulgur*, although etymologically it comes from late Latin, *relamptare*, which is "to shine".' Such was his knowledge of Latin. She had a gulp of water and there came a noise – a very loud noise – from inside her. As though her body were a drum, for a few brief seconds the rumbling noise occupied her entirely, all the way from her ears to her feet. She then looked in the direction of the windows overlooking the canal and for the second time saw the man who had that ambassadorial look about him; alone at a table, he had his eyes closed and was draining the last of a bottle of mineral water. At that moment, his body was also completely atremor.

She remembered standing looking at souvenirs and post-cards in a shop, and buying a black-and-white postcard, in which a shot of Venice from the air had the look of a mountain chain, with its snowy peaks, its rivers and its forests, and him breaking the silence to say: 'The millions of tree trunks down in the mud beneath the city, holding it up while at the same time dragging it under, are all offerings of condolence. As if, at the moment it was founded, Venice sent itself millions of condolence messages for the future. A buried trunk for every inhabitant.' It was starting to rain heavily when they reached the last bridge on the final stretch back to the palazzo. At the highest point on the arch, she looked back and had the sensation that they were sinking, subsiding into the earth, never to be seen again.

On another of those days, they went to St Mark's Square in the morning; they knew it was still cordoned off because of the unexplained sound-vacuum bubble, which was continuing to have a severe effect on anyone who dared cross it, but they only wanted to go and see it as it was now, not a single footprint marring the snow-covered, completely unpeopled space. They spent the later part of the day again trying to reach the gardens that held the Biennale, that prestigious exhibition in which numerous westernized countries had their own pavilions, built at some point in the previous century in accordance with patriotic styles and nationalistic cultural topics. The writer and her husband knew they would all be closed, the Biennale not being held that year, but neither of them minded; to them, seeing the constructions from outside was special enough. It was all set within a forest on the eastern edge of the city, not the most inviting place after nightfall, but in any case the couple miscalculated the distance and failed to even get close; no boats go that way after 7 p.m. in winter. Once they were back at the palazzo, he spent a few minutes sitting on the sofa contemplating the blue pulsations coming from Alexa's heart – they were yet to use the device – when she, on the armchair, deep in their city guidebook, looked up and said, 'Can you imagine Latin never having existed?' 'What?' he said, not taking his eye off the blue pulsations. 'Yes, the idea of Latin, the language you know so well, being an imaginary language, a language we're heading towards – not the one we come from, but something painstakingly designed for the day when everyone comes to speak it.'

Then the day came when he confessed that something was troubling him, something he had not told her about and that was gnawing away at him, which had happened on their visit to the record shop: 'While you were looking at the American No Wave records, I'd almost finished in the classical section when, without knowing it – I was still immersed in the cover of the Chopin record – I found myself at the back of the shop, and there was a man there, tall, elegantly turned out, blue suit, silvery hair, and he said to me to go through, not to be afraid, and then he asked if I wanted to record something, but not the usual kind of thing, something genuinely unique, and said there was another room where he had everything you needed to record special records like that – that was how he put it, *special records*. I didn't know what to say – I went with him. We crossed an interior courtyard full of plants and caged birds, pigeons, seagulls, everyday birds like that – it made me think of Noah's Ark – and then we went into a hut with some steps inside which led down to an underground room: the walls were blue, and it was brightly lit and had a welcoming feel to it, and there were microphones hanging down everywhere from the ceiling. On one side there was a floor-to-ceiling glass panel looking through to the control room, which had nobody in it. And the man said to me to go and stand in the middle of the room, under the cloud of microphones, and then he came and stood next to me, and took my hand, squeezing it gently but at the same time with a firmness, and told me to say something, go on, he said, say something, before all the sounds on earth are erased, time's running out, he said, and I laughed, and he closed his eyes and squeezed my hand harder and again said, "Time's running out, time's running out," and I was starting to feel very jumpy now and I said something but I actually don't even know what because from that moment on there's a blank in my memory, a total blank, until the moment I found myself in the other room, the control room on the other side of the glass, and the man, who throughout all of this was extremely polite with me, and at this point still not having let go of my hand, showed me something, an object on a table, I couldn't tell what it was at first, a black sphere the size of a basketball made of a very tough-looking material: it glinted in the artificial light. And he said, "You can touch it, don't be afraid," and I let go of his hand and went over to the sphere, but it was giving off heat, a lot of heat, a wet sort of heat, as though there was something alive and sweating inside it, so I didn't touch it. "It's vinyl," he said, "a perfect vinyl sphere, it's just come out of the oven." And indeed, it smelled like it had just been made; if everything new-made briefly has an unfamiliar smell about it, imagine what *this* thing was like. And then he said: "Open it." "What do you mean, open it?" "Just that," he said, "open it." But I wasn't going near it, so he put his hand on it and it literally just fell apart, into a multitude of slices, which he quickly cupped in his hands around so that they wouldn't fall apart entirely; he pressed it back together, into its original spherical shape again. "As you'll have guessed by now," he said, "it's a sphere made up of thousands of vinyl records, as though, starting from the North Pole, someone had cut the Earth up into millions of slices, until they reached the South Pole. There are so many slices of vinyl in this sphere that we don't even try to find out how many; each of them is a record in which the grooves on the A-side fit perfectly with those of the next record's B-side, as though they were each other's negatives, and it goes on like that until they make up a perfect sphericity of sounds." Completely perplexed, I looked at the thing. The records, logically enough, were wider the closer you went to the Equator, thinner closer to the North and South Poles, so thin that I thought they must only be able to hold a single sound at most, a simple phoneme or a single piano note in the case that it was music which had been recorded. When you joined all the records, the surfaces of the grooves indeed fitted together like they were moulds for a perfect cosmos, and you felt that there was a force inside them, a real and inexplicable tension, "It encloses an infinite three-dimensional sound," said the man, while I, still feeling quite uneasy and not having said anything, simply looked at him. "There's a whole world in there," he went on, "surely you can feel it? We call it the spherical record, or simply The Sphere; the sonic richness it contains and the storage capacity is absolute. Look how beautiful each of the spiralling grooves is, the way the needle must advance, irremediably, towards the centre of each record, an advance like the spirals on snail shells or sea conches, like those on stairways in people's dreams and inside our ear canals. The spiral is the only thing that, each time it comes around, returns to the same place without ever returning to the same place." Then he brought over a kind of microscope, and, taking one of the records from the sphere at random, put it under the lens and beckoned me to have a look. I couldn't help but exclaim – its surface looked like the Himalayas seen from the air, the vision revealed a hugely rich landscape of troughs and peaks, and of what appeared to be rivers, too, and vegetation and different colours, colours above all, which truly left me so bewildered I thought it had to be a joke, a magic trick, something he amused himself with, fooling unsuspecting customers like me. "Lovely, isn't it?" he said. "The thing is, everything you see down there is your voice, everything contained in this sphere is what you, with the two of us holding hands, have just recorded in the booth. It took you no more than five minutes to record it and yet a whole lifetime wouldn't be enough to listen to it back." And then I suddenly felt afraid, very afraid, and I rushed out of there, came up from that subterranean complex and went and found you – you were still busy in the No Wave section – though first of all, I heard that man say from behind me, "Come back for the sphere whenever you want, it's yours, we'll keep it here for you." Naturally, I haven't.'

Until a day came when they heard the volume go up in the usually quiet street outside, neighbours speaking across their balconies, and gondoliers and skippers of motorboats seemingly communicating in shouts. The couple had made coffee and while they ate a breakfast of sweet Venetian pastries, they turned on the television; it was being reported on a local channel that not only was St Mark's Square itself cordoned off now, but the security perimeter had been extended by 100 metres all around it after that pocket of total soundlessness had been found to be causing not only strong headaches but also blindness, in certain cases irreversibly. But as well as the absence of sounds and the blindness, there was now no smell there either; a thing so extraordinary that no human could be said to be prepared to experience it. They turned off the television, spread the map out on the table and came up with a way of getting to the Biennale complex – the only significant tourist destination they still had not been able to visit – that would avoid the cordoned-off areas but nonetheless be as direct as possible; the route they sketched out would entail an unlikely combination of sections on foot and others by gondola and motorboat. They set off, again passing the house with the statue on its façade whose eyes had been taken out – the male writer dropped his gaze, again struck by the incomprehensibility of such vandalism. After half an hour, as they passed the food market, they witnessed an accident. A taxi boat and a boat with an outboard motor crashed into one another, seemingly for no reason; moments later a third vessel, coming up from behind, then crashed into the first two, before bursting into flames. Boats and gondolas swarmed around, everyone trying to help, several individuals even taking out what appeared to be business cards and handing them to the people involved in the crash; maybe, he said, they were lawyers offering their services on a commission basis. Between the noise of the swell and all the shouting, they heard somebody say that the people involved were blind, all blind. The couple decided to go back to the palazzo. They walked in complete silence. The sun went behind a cloud; she did up the top pearly black button on her blouse to cover her neck. A few hours later, while she, sitting in the living room, looked out across the domes of St Mark's Basilica, he broke the silence to say: 'There is a way to avoid crashing, a very simple one: if you suddenly find yourself about to crash, and you intentionally turn the steering wheel in the direction of the collision, you'll go *towards* the collision, and when you reach the point it's taking place, the cars involved won't be there any more, they will already be somewhere different in the road. A rule that actually applies to lots of things, conflicts between nations included, and between couples, too.' She looked pensive for a moment: 'But this idea of needing to turn towards the collision to save yourself,' she said, 'are you trying to tell me something with that?' 'Yes, I'm trying to tell you that we should go and jump over the police cordon and go out into the middle of St Mark's Square. We should go towards the place where everything is being erased. It's the only way to save ourselves.'

But they didn't go, they didn't so much as approach St Mark's Square that day because the following one marked end of their holiday. They were due to leave very early, and packed their bags and got ready after supper so they could be sure to catch the first vaporetto to the airport. She was woken at dawn by him shouting in the living room. Throwing back the sheets, she rushed through; still in his pyjamas, her husband was pointing at a collection of large boxes in a pile. 'I was coming to make coffee when I saw them,' he said. They were both dumbstruck. He went over to the boxes, she begged him not to touch them, but, bending down, he opened one; it was empty. She recoiled – he then opened another box, which was empty too, and another and another, until it became clear that none of them had anything in them. She went back to the bedroom, threw on her clothes, not even brushing her hair, checked the clock, dragged the suitcases through to the living room, where he, still in his pyjamas, stood staring at the empty boxes in silence. 'What are you doing just standing there? Get dressed, come on.' He seemed not to hear her until, coming out of his reverie, he said: 'I'm going to stay, I'm going to stay, a dream can become reality, I finally see, and this dream's trying to tell me something, the men in the dream weren't here to bring us something, quite the opposite, they came to ask for something, and what they are asking is that I complete their dream, that I be the one to bring the rest of it to life, that I myself fill up their empty boxes, I think they even want me to help bring *them* to life, to turn them into flesh and bone, I see clearly that this is what I need to do, I don't know how but I have to, however long it takes, this is my mission in Venice, you can go to Montevideo, see to the house, I'll be here, come back whenever you want.'

II.

The best place to hide something is in the fire. (*Fire love*)

The clotheslines out on the patio have become tangled in the wind. The tangle has created a knot; it's the same shape as your sex.
   – she says.
I've seen it. This valley we've been walking also has the same shape as the floor of the ocean that once covered it.
   – he says.

Another way of understanding things is to say that we come from a darkness and are moving towards another darkness. Between the two there is only a brief candle, a match pointlessly struck, although everyone's soul gets its corporate branding in the end. (*Match love*)

It's as though the world has become a skin that's been turned inside out and, having never previously seen the light, is still fresh and steaming, bloody even, laid open for all to see.
   – he says.
A language we must invent where there's nothing. The intangible business of survival.
   – she says.

The infinity of ad breaks on television only dawns on you when, watching a movie à la carte, the ads come on and you skip through them in time-lapse, and it seems like the slowest time-lapse in the world; the promotional images you once enjoyed watching now seem to you if not dead then dying. When a couple splits up, each of them goes back through the experience, also in time-lapse, and the exact opposite happens: the advert of their coexistence, so to speak, appears. Moments of boredom in their daily routine, moments that at the time manifested as pointless addenda or bound-to-be-forgotten detritus, but that now, in the succession of images coming back to you, reveal themselves to be as muscular as a grasshopper's hind legs, as beautiful as a rhizome's impossible root, infinite like the balance of the credit cards in dreams; detritus, all of it, in which – precisely, right there in the detritus – you feel that a cell, however small, could have existed of the thing we call 'union'. (*Advert love*)

Every night, while you sleep, your eyelids are the sluice gates of a river that stop me from swimming back up your body, from entering you. Outside, meanwhile, the valley awaits the sun in darkness, and I spend the time thinking of its perpetual snow and of the nameless birds who in that moment will be cutting through the air above it. At times, this sort of mineral silence gives rise to a noise that excavates the darkness, leaving it not only shorn of its silence but riddled, hollow.

– she says.

Hollow space filled with fears and solitude, hollow space for all the surplus, the overspill, the remainders. Noise is only music we don't yet understand.

– he says.

The speeches of politicians and orators, and their associated powers of persuasion, have nothing to do with the words they use, but rather with the music inherent in those words. Hitler is a succession of *fortississimos*, Churchill an alternation of *fortissimo/piano*. Fidel Castro oscillates between *pianissimo* and *mezzo forte* – an oscillation with no discernible pattern – while JFK is a continuous *mezzo piano* with the occasional *subito piano* thrown in, and so on. What becomes clear, therefore, is this one truth: leaders do not relate to the masses through the semantics of their words but via the secret musical score within which these words are inscribed and modulated. This is also demonstrated by the tweets exchanged by leading government officials, in which it is not the words but rather the intensity, intonation, rhythm and imagined prosody that are the thing. Inversely, these other things we commonly call 'songs', and which play on radios and stereos, have nothing to do with music, they are words and musical notes that end up metamorphosing into the leaders' voices, into the true texts of power; the music used at rallies and at 'free' raves and that you hear being piped in at large department stores are also clear examples of this. But the love between two people, which as such has to be modulated by an original tune that is theirs and theirs alone, comes about when it is impossible to conceive of a device – analogue, manual or electronic – capable of recording and registering the music that comes from the lovers' mouths. Love is the loss of one's own voice with no possibility of it being reinvented as something called power. (*Unrecordable love*)

The moon is up already.
  – he says, at breakfast.
Stepping on her, demeaning her to the point of subjugation, made no difference to her ancestral instinct for

supplanting the sun. Nor to our union.
    – she says.

Up to a certain age, at some point between 40 and 50, the thing we call 'pain' is the product of impetuous excitement, of being daring and of a certain kind of passion. This pain is then substituted by another, very different kind, which comes from degradation, illness and solitude. By this we do not mean a cosmic solitude but rather a political solitude, because your relationship with the cosmos is always inevitably a good one – death and its natural processes attest to the harmony of this pact – unlike that with the ruling class, which, as you grow older, reveals its predictability and can only generate in any human a sensation of abandonment and, finally, a desire to break with every administrative tie. This, pain's trajectory, is the same as love's trajectory, only that it goes in reverse; as though its intention were to neutralize it. Leading in the end to a zero sum. (*Neutralization love*)

When I enter and exit the groove between your buttocks, my skin comes from another world.
    – he says.
To love has nothing to do with looking up at the heavens and feeling stupefied by the gods' demands. To love means looking down and using the tip of your tongue to write in the orifice of desire.
    – she says.

At certain times, in places where photography is prohibited for whatever reason, there is no option but to look up and take photographs of the sky. Climate-dependent, blue or light grey rectangles will appear, or also the white of clouds or a nocturnal black; empty spaces, all. Trying to spot previously seen figures in empty spaces is a recurrent theme. Mediums do it with the Bélmez Faces, radiologists do it with X-rays, and experts and enthusiasts alike do it when contemplating abstract oil paintings. Extreme cases are grouped under the term 'apophenia': 'the tendency to perceive meaningful connections between unrelated things'. But the world is one huge copyright now, every-thing protected and actionable, leaving the normal citizen with no option but to look up and take photos of the sky. It happens in theme parks and in museums too – where the ceilings are the only thing you are allowed to point a camera at – and it is beginning to happen in city streets as well. A day will come when all we have of our urban spaces will be images of the skies above them, and, like somebody divining the past in the viscera of a freshly killed bison, we will be left to remember the city via the cloud that presided over it or the name of the bird tra-versing its airspace. Love is precisely this, the definitive apophenia, noise+interpretation, a mark that appears out of nothing and upon which we confer, with unshake-able certainty, a comprehensible shape – a shape also about to fade into another that is not only unknown to us but that we will never succeed in knowing. (*Apophenia love*)

On the night of the Great Blackout, you were untouched by the flames not because you aren't made of flesh and bone – you are, I can attest to that – but because you live on the very outer shore of time.
  – she says.

It takes skill to stay one step ahead of sundials. The sun is a star which burns everyone.

– he says.

It is normal that, in trying to make a better life for ourselves, we guess at the future, something that ultimately comes down to simple cause and effect, which we use every day and which can be described as *understanding past and present allows us to predict what will happen tomorrow*. But it is no less true that without the risk inherent in all that is present – in things happening at this very moment, live and direct – there is no vibration to move our lives or our vital powers, and so we could also test out this other formula that does not look to the future but rather, precisely, to the present: *we try to understand past and future in an attempt to predict today*. Or in other words, to imagine a future in combination with what we know about the past in order to act in the here and now. Or, more clearly still: instead of anticipating futures that will never arrive and that have a mortgaging effect on the present moment, to see that the present resides not only in what we have left behind but also in what is ahead of us. The vegetal image applies perfectly here: the tree now producing fruit – real fruit, fruit you can chew in your mouth and consume – does so because of the flower it once gave forth and because that fruit will eventually become something inedible, something rotten. This and only this is why we are able to experience and touch with our hands the one thing we will never completely know, the here and now. Love – that which is radically alive – is this here and now, but projected spherically, in all directions. (*Present love*)

I went to the start of the valley today. By some miracle, there are still a few buildings left standing, though they're derelict. Weeds are growing up inside them and out through the roofs.

    – she says.

I've seen them, and a poster too, just as badly damaged, which says: 'When it snows, birds come here.'

    – he says.

No love exists that bears inside it the negation of love. When you say 'love', the person you are speaking to need not have any special thoughts in order to receive this word with genuine admiration. In the same way that in the sciences energy is always a positive sign (except for in virtual tricks, there is no such thing as negative energy), when we speak about it, love always appears as a positively superior entity, something that goes unquestioned as it penetrates the person who hears it, just as symbols of divine entities do. Illustrations of the Virgin Mary, of Coca-Cola, of tax-collection agencies or the Buddha never seem deformed or shapeless, and we overlook any spelling mistakes they contain or blemishes on their faces or bald heads, and the reason for this supposed beauty and perfection is simple: by adoring them so much we have succeeded in erasing any hint of real life in them, turning them into objects, abstract symbols, empty containers. To be more specific: it is not that tax-collection agencies or the Buddha are adored in themselves, but rather that the images of those agencies or the Buddha are adored – now becoming symbols from which all trace of ugliness has been removed, and any criticism of which will get you banished from your community. Nonetheless, love still performs a monumental function: it gives us the idea that not all is lost, it breathes life into the hope that in some far-off future, and in the manner of telefilms with their happy endings, history will redeem all our missteps, for example the one that makes us adore people, animals and symbols that no longer exist. And this is precisely the fiction that, minute by minute, and with true assiduousness, couples try in vain to create, in anticipation of the day when everything comes to an end: to create a love that goes beyond the adoration of the symbols the two of them patiently invent and that, finally, they will also cold-heartedly destroy. (*Symbol love*)

I know my love for you is unlike any love I've felt before because in every square centimetre of your body I encounter you wholly. I lick this minutia off you and all that you are moves inside me.
   – she says.
The passion we share has nothing to do with this valley we now inhabit, nor with the stations of the sun running swiftly over our heads, and still less with a fantasy of shared eternity; our passion is to do with that tongue-twisting machine you lick every night.
   – he says.

What happens between the moment of somebody being born and their dying is not what they experience but what they do not experience, what goes unexperienced. What has been experienced is already done, definitively lost, or in the best case has become the property of others. But it is no less true that these things that still remain for us to do were already contained in our first minute of life, and comprise an absence that, with all the power of a Prime

Mover, have been with us in every moment of our lives, and in fact, though they have never manifested, are what make our lives real and believable. Hence the way a dead person's face can suddenly look like a stone to us, or the face of someone who never existed: in this moment it's what we *haven't* experienced that emigrates, that departs the body forever. There is some similarity between this and waking from a dream, briefly remembering one's dream as though it had been real, then forgetting it utterly, but being left for the rest of that day, if not longer, with a neutral flavour, some ongoing aridity, the roughness of a mask or stone. (*Prime Mover love*)

I sometimes feel an urge to open up your chest, the hair on it so transparent it can't even be seen, and plunge my hands into your heart. To find the key to this valley made from our bodies.
  – she says.
Your chest is a precious stone, its hardness brooks no doubt.
  – he says.

Every certainty taken to the limits of that certainty leads us to total doubt. Inversely, every doubt taken to the limits of that doubt leads us to absolute certainty. So it is with love. (*Limit love*)

How many years has it been since we saw anyone?
  – he says.
You and I are as a whole host.
  – she says.

There is a square in the city of Venice with an old fountain in it. In the middle of the fountain is a monument
to a hero of the city. Two pipes lead from the fountain,
pouring water into a lake. Each of these pipes is a small
sculpture of a dog with the water coming out of its mouth.
Animals that do not drink water but rather emit it, vomit
it out, so to speak. It is an old idea, this one about fauna
whose bodies do the opposite of what's expected: the
dream of creatures that do things backwards. For example,
these pictures of half-beasts, half-humans found so frequently in mythologies old and new. The domestication
of animals, always something imperfect, always a projection – and nowadays having reached an end point in the
household pet – is a response to the mechanism of the
animal that behaves in a manner exactly opposite to its
nature. Something about love recalls those two dogs on a
fountain in Venice that have spent centuries backwardly
inventing nature. (*Animals-that-do-things-backwards love*)

The first phrase I learned in Latin was *Columbae aquam
potant*. When pigeons still had names and drank water.
Today the only thing left of this phrase is the water.
    – he says.
No library replicates the real world, nor far less this unknown world.
    – she says.

When wood and silence are joined together, the silence
is expelled and more wood created: utensils, machines,
combustibles, cellulose – all of which go out across the
world making their own noise. But, above all, the origins
of wood and silence go back to the origins of humanity

too: raw material for the wheel and fire, which are things that, every time they are used, do make the noise of a new love, a previously unheard chord. (*Noise love*)

The first phrase I learned in Latin was *Omnes non moriuntur*, not everybody dies.
– he says.
If you don't die, neither will I.
– she says.

You don't forget the films you watch on aeroplanes, but you also don't remember them as fully as the ones you watch on land; rather, they get mixed up into one single film. This may be to do with the lack of oxygen you experience 10,000 kilometres up in the air, combined with the always inexact cabin pressure, an unnatural combination that alters your perception of images. Or we might resort to mythology and say that Icarus, on his ascent to the perennial fire of the sun, also confused real and imaginary love in a single image, and that, as he then tried to establish which was which, he melted like wax. But we might also say that within the delays to every aeroplane cutting through the skies at this moment in time, there lies the alternative history of humanity. (*Delay love*)

Sometimes, not thinking about anything in particular, I go along the valley, following the ocean of stars above my head, and then I am walking a different valley. I come across different plants, previously unknown minerals, previously untouched animals. Or the eucalyptuses, such fast trees, unrivalled among plants, growing at a rate of a metre a year – like you and me.

– she says.

Love also appears when, absentmindedly, brazenly, we tread on somebody else's soul and they don't complain.

– he says.

Illness is also a part of health. A healthy person is only the permanently teetering equilibrium between the tendency to be well or unwell. This is like saying that death forms part of life, and that the opposite of life is not death, but nothingness. Or, taking it further: we have two bodies – one living, one dead – that coexist in our flesh. A never-ending process. (*Illness love*)

The night plays tricks on me: the trees grow upwards and sink down, the perpetual snow shakes like water in its liquid state, the darkness is an unknown animal, as unknown as the nameless bird that came and landed on our windowsill after the Great Blackout.

– he says.

It's my body, not the world, that's playing tricks.

– she says.

If the metaphor is, by definition, the object that contains within it an infinity of other objects, money is the perfect metaphor; the most poetic object in existence. A €20 note has the potential to contain all and everything in the universe whose value is understood to be between €1 and €20. Or indeed, between €0.10 and €20. Or indeed, between €0.01 and €20. Or indeed, between €0.0001 and

€20. The regress to €0 is infinite in the strict sense; in fact, this zero-euro value will never be reached because the thing worth zero cannot be bought; it falls outside the money-metaphor's field of action. Every humanist tradition posits certain things ungoverned by money, that it cannot buy – love, for example, the universe, human life or a nearly extinct species of animal – not because they have a zero value, but entirely the opposite: because their value is infinite, because they are so valuable that no price can be put on them. But it is also true that nothing prevents us from positing human life, the universe, a nearly extinct species of animal or love as having no value for precisely the opposite reason: they *are* the zero that money can neither reach nor, therefore, buy. These two stances, the one that 'goes upwards' – to the infinite price of things that are important – and the one that 'goes downwards' – to the zero price of these same things – divide the history of thought, and economics, and religion, the arts and sciences, and, in short, humanity itself – creating two irreconcilable poles. This therefore allows for such questions as: what kind of love is produced by having a zero price? Is it the same love as that produced by an infinite price? Do these two loves produce similar experiences and visions of the love object? Or, on the contrary, does the love derived from having a zero price create a totally distinct image of the love object? And if so, what is this new love object like when seen moving around, when you look them in the eye, when you see them eat, urinate, laugh or kiss, when they are either being penetrated or doing the penetrating? Does this new class of love object engender the feeling of levitation we experience when lovestruck? Or do we perhaps see in them a previously unseen darkness, the zero-grade absence of light, something unique that, being so extremely singular, for the time that it lasts cannot *but* be loved? In summary, is this new love – arrived at after reaching its zero price – some unprecedented being, a monster never before seen or imagined, a creature that, if we were able to look at it, would *ipso facto* result in our death from fright and pleasure, horror and ecstasy, perfect hate and perfect union? We do not know – we do not know what it would be like to contemplate this kind of love derived from a zero price, from this aberration in standard logic, but we speculate that it will be something very similar to the way we nowadays think about the dead, about stones, plants and animals. An entire class of amorous relationship we have yet to give form to. The love felt by that which is pure and absolutely unknown towards humans. The love of the radically *other*. (*Zero love*)

Him, with naked fingers inside the naked cavity:
Your body is a river.
Her, in a posture so commonplace that it evokes a kind of happiness taken to be eternal:
This river has its source in you.

If we were to mix up all the shadows of the trees in a city or a forest, and the shadow of every blade of grass and of the passers-by and the buildings, so that not all the shadows were pointing towards the same cardinal point, we don't know what this would lead to; not what the resultant landscape would be like, nor how our minds would go about dealing with such a roulette of darknesses. When any kind of doubt enters into the love between two people, the emotional landscape that then settles in is somewhat akin to this roulette of shadows. (*Non-cardinal love*)

In the days that followed the Great Blackout, we found men, women and children all over the place. Although they lay dead, they were all still different from one another, just as different as they had been in life.

– he says.

A dead person is an ecosystem marked by a question with no answer: what was the last thing they dreamed? Dead people are different from one another not because they were different in life, but because at the moment of death each of them held within them their final dream, a dream that goes on continually unfolding and growing inside the dead body.

– she says.

Counter to the widely held belief, an actor's profession does not consist of interpreting different characters, but in dying onstage. Acting is the art of dying again and again. In an anonymous poem, an elegy for Shakespeare published in the First Folio, someone wrote: 'An actor's art' is to 'die, and live, to act a second part'. And love constitutes a stage performance of a particular kind; actors and actresses fall in love on screen as many times as they have to. Having said this, in life outside the theatre and beyond the screen, it is well known that the act of love is linked to death for a simple reason: the intention to love is always the intention to melt or dissolve into a body not your own; to die, ultimately. Indeed, the one doing the loving wishes to die inside the beloved, although said desire is never realized, and after making love we come back to life again, as many times as we have to, and keep on trying. In its own way, this repetition of love in our lives is a job, though an unpaid one. We will go further still and say that this and only this is the work truly proper to humans, and puts real-life love on a level with the love we see feigned on screens, in novels, in poetry and in all the stories we've been told since childhood. (*Work love*)

If you tripped over that granite block in front of us and fell, which side would you rather your body landed on?
     – he says, on one of their long walks on the side of the mountain where the house is situated, so long that they could be qualified as expeditions, pointing to a stone.
My left side, the same side Joan of Arc landed on when she fell scorched from the pyre.
     – she says, still looking at her feet, with an answer he thought he did not entirely understand.

Examining the Thaddäus Haenke herbariums that have been conserved in several different European museums, but above all the ones from the catalogues of his garden in the Cochabamba hacienda, we see the flowers and plants are attached to brown paper with a rudimentary kind of sticky tape he invented. We also find many different fruits in the shape of pears and mangos – disintegrated now due to dehydration – which Haenke tried to prevent from coming undone by tying them up with string, like packages or postcards that have taken three centuries to reach us. Sticky tape and string, eternal and nevertheless moribund tools uniting us with chlorophyll. (*String love*)

How can there be a forest without humans? The forest is a human invention, a pre-human forest is impossible.
     – he says.

When the sounds of forest and city reach the same timbre, tone and volume, in that precise moment, your body and mine are also the same note.
  – she says.

You could create a portrait, whether in writing or pictorially, of everything you see in the street or in your home: a portrait of the table you eat at and of the ceiling you look up at every night when you go to bed, of the cup you drink from and the traffic lights you stop at, and of the tap in the sink and the plug on standby next to the record player; you could even go inside each of these objects, for example said plug, and see close-up for the first time the forward movement of a screw's spiral and the colour of an internal plastic part and the cable connections, and you could also follow the course of these cables until you eventually came out at a power station situated in the other part of the world, yes, this and much more you could explore and document and you would always come to the same conclusion: all these objects have, printed or otherwise marked on them, the manufacturer's name, the name of something that the objects are not. You live inside commercial brands, in the gestation of their mythologies and legends. You are the foetus of the big corporations. 'Corporation' comes from 'corpus' – yours. (*Corporation love*)

I live in the shadow of your body, soft as a flame.
  – he says.
It isn't true that the stars shine on us. We are the light that begins inside them, the power we possess, properly considered, is of them. Power enough to take the fear of the

other and shatter it into a thousand pieces every single night.
   – she says.

In the case that a Last Judgement did exist, it could only be arbitrated by the one truly final thing we know, love. Love would be witness, prosecutor, defence, accused and judge. Carefully considered, this is a way of describing the theatre of every breakup – the comedy of judgement – acted out by the lovers. (*Last Judgement love*)

In the first epoch of our life in this house – which was a long, long time ago, since to my mind we have passed a great many epochs between these four walls – when you went out onto the mountainside for food, or to defecate between those two rocks that hold the curvature of your buttocks better than even my hands do, or when you were simply going out to look across the perpetual snow, you always glanced at yourself in the mirror by the door. And your face would remain there, flat and still, with no degradation or loss of detail, and I could look at it until evening.
   – he says.
Since the Great Blackout, mirrors have held memory. The last and hopeless reserve of light.
   – she says.

All bodies open up a gap in the air. All bodies are empty spaces in the air that have flourished, become something. When taking soil samples, geologists extract long cylinders of earth, clay, ice and stones, which, ordered by strata, indicate the terrestrial age of the hole. There are also layers and strata from every epoch inside us – since we are ultimately cylinders of meat, fat and water, but blended and shuffled together in a complex network that we never fully understand. It would seem that the principal node of this bodily network is love. And there is a logic to this. If not, like a block of ice in the sun, we would have melted various aeons ago: extinct layers of neglect and sorrow. (*Principal-node love*)

I sometimes think that by loving one another so intensely, by this unending thirst to enter and exit all of each other's cavities, what we are doing is training our souls.
   – she says.
For the day the light comes back.
   – he says.

Killing someone is sometimes a crime and sometimes an act of heroism. Kill someone in civil society, and you pay for it in jail; kill that same person in a war, and a medal awaits you. This would seem to suggest that killing is not a thing in and of itself, but rather an act which, depending on *where it comes from*, will be qualified as either unforgivable or worthy of applause. Death at somebody else's hands is, then, something directional, a veritable vector; one that not only has an intensity, but also a direction and a meaning. This apparent paradox pertains in many different ambits. A black key on a piano always makes the same sound, but anyone who knows about music theory can tell you that this key can be a different note – flat or sharp – depending on the note that precedes it: depending on *where the melody comes from*, we will have a different musical note – C sharp or D flat, for example – though the same note has been played. Killing oneself is another example: do so on a Formula One racetrack, and you will immediately be elevated to hero status; do it by smoking cigarettes, and you are relegated to social detritus. And all of this speaks to us of the concept of staging. It is the stage – the setting in which an action takes place – that confers meaning on the action, modifying it irrevocably. It is not for nothing that we speak of a 'theatre of operations' in war, where killing is licit, but never in relation to terrorism or deaths that occur in peacetime. This indicates that war and theatre, though diametrically different as activities, are structurally identical. We see the same principle at work in love and hate: what distinguishes them is the context, the place either is coming from. Hence we sometimes hear speak of that utter impossibility known as love-hate. (*Directional love*)

When you arrive in a place for the first time, it's bad luck if the first piece of writing you see is something somebody else has written. As soon as we arrived in this valley, I saw your name written in the soil. I'd scratched it there with a stick.
    – she says.
And it's still there. No kind of luck exists – good or bad – that can do away with your handwriting.
    – he says.

In the film *An Unmarried Woman*, a woman having supper with her female friends sighs and says she misses the 'old-fashioned highball orgasm'. When a couple breaks up, this is the nature of the theatre – the simulation of the Final Judgement – on show. (*Old-fashioned highball orgasm love*)

Sunsets here don't languish like fish out of water. On the contrary, they light us up more and more as the light fades.
    – he says.
We are the silver and ruby that shine in the eyes of the fireflies.
    – she says.

To say nothing of the classic theme of painter and model. On the scale of planetary history and its transformations – a scale subject to a time so vast that we call it *deep time* – the fossils studied by palaeobotanists show that plants survive all kinds of catastrophes and animal extinctions; plants survive on a scale so massive that we as humans cannot fully comprehend it. The habitual preoccupation with the way in which humans are affecting the evolution of plant life is thus only a primitive and wrongheaded projection of another, totally different phenomenon, one we are able to see because it belongs to our temporal scale and affects us directly: the gradual extinction of diversity in human cultures due to the globalizing effect of world commerce and advertising, an extinction that – on the other hand – is subject to a short time span, human time, a time infinitesimally small if we compare it with that other, vegetal time. By copying a model of time applicable only to the love we profess for one another, we create a useless sort of deep time. (*Anthropocene love*)

The city expels its dead. Like an evil accompanying the coming of a flood, it empties them into the fields beyond the final houses, depositing them in a place that cannot even be considered the outskirts.

– he says.

You and I are that place, and we aren't dead.

– she says.

Love is questioned with the same persistency and hostility with which company logos, folk dances, the burning of books or the destruction of Our Lady of Fátima's image are questioned. The motive being nothing other than the fact that such destructions would lay bare what lies behind all these things: nothing, or at least nothing of what is generally assumed. (*Logo love*)

I thought I heard footsteps last night, they came from the track in the valley, they approached the house, they prowled around it.

– he says.

Don't worry, it was me, it was my predator-body, which had materialized. My love-body was still at your side, watching over you.

– she says.

As for love with non-humans, the key moment, the point of no return, is the creation of emotional ties with objects that will always be separate from us: machines and animals. These are attempts to create love from places we have no access to: from death – the computer – and from non-human life – the animal elevated to pet. If we analyze these two, the first, rhetorically known as Artificial Intelligence, comprises our dream of assembling love from inert parts, of giving life to the conjoined assemblage of inanimate objects; the second is the dream of using simple animal flesh to generate a creature similar to us, a human almost always in the shape of a dog or cat. The key, and what reveals these impossibilities for what they are, is to understand that though computers and pets hear us, they do not listen to us. Nonetheless, there is an alternative to impossible loves such as these, and it requires a complete recasting of the love impulse and the creation of a kind of love of that which is genuinely accessible; this we could call a *love of what is sufficient*. It would consist in simply accepting and being satisfied with things as they are, *satisfied* in the etymological sense. *Satis*, 'enough' + *facere*, 'to make'. (*Sufficient love*)

When I pick up pencil and paper, I am unable to draw my hand without it also being yours.
    – he says.
And this valley has the same shape as the floor of the ocean that once covered it.
    – she says.

The maximum number of days you can go without liquids before dying of dehydration is the same number of days you can go without sleep before irreversibly losing your mind, three. It might therefore be said that sleep and water share a common symbol: the stream. And that would be true were it not for the fact that water descends due to the influence of gravitational acceleration, whereas sleep, unsusceptible to that tug, rises upwards, and goes on rising upwards until a second and more significant difference appears: sleep never stops, there is no ocean that can arrest it nor lake into which it might flow. Where water particles want to descend, to be more water and join together with others of their kind, sleep wants to rise, to be itself and only itself. None of which prevents there being a great proliferation of images of water and sleep when two lovers come together over a divorce contract and discuss the differences between what they would like the new animal called separation to be and what it really is: the continuation of love via the means of conflict. (*Divorce love*)

When we copulate, it is an animal with a single direction.
    – she says.
Hand-in-hand, through the dark streets, after the Great Blackout we tried to find the path of a kind of sex that by then was virtually non-existent, the seismic kind.
    – he says.

VENICE (2)

The writer taps away, as we've said, there is a nervous energy to her striking of the typewriter's keys, she has barely slept in days, the snow globe on the desk shakes, making it snow in the miniature version of the city whose canals Lord Byron boasted of having swum in winter, the city that was the birthplace of the butcher who in later centuries would be Charles Manson's inspiration, whose prisons Giacomo Casanova escaped and in whose waters Richard Wagner drowned, the city where the first bank cheque was signed and capitalism invented, the city at whose Lido Goethe collected hundreds of conches, the city with its Marciana Library, where there is a cache of unpublished lines by Petrarch, the city with which that greatest explorer of the East, Freya Stark, fell in love, the city Galileo Galilei came to detest, and on the writer goes, tapping away, while in this labyrinth of tourists and water and stone the early summer humidity is ushering in a storm, and she counts the number of words she types between lightning flash and thunder crack, and every time there are fewer of them and all and only about the one subject of interest to her, love. Pausing her writing, she turns her mind to her husband, asleep in the next room; he lies prone beside a large sphere made of vinyl which, as though it were a totem, he has placed on an improvised pedestal on the nightstand.

She recalls the journey of a few days before from Montevideo to Venice. She remembers falling asleep in her seat while looking out at the curvature of the plane's wingtip. With the lights off inside the cabin, the small bulbs marking the emergency exits had seemed like flames burning in a temple, and then at one point she was woken by a movement in the seat next to her, which had been empty before, followed by a noise not made by the plane itself, a noise like when you wake in the night and cannot get back to sleep, and you lie there listening to the breathing of the person asleep beside you, and she remembers having opened her eyes completely and seeing, there beside her, silently staring at the seatback in front of him, the man who looked like an ambassador and in turn reminded her of a Berber who many years before had split into two people and disappeared into the Atlas Mountains. She glanced around at the other seats in the tail section; all empty. To her surprise, the man struck up a conversation with her, 'Are you travelling alone?' 'Yes...' she paused, 'my husband is waiting for me in Venice,' before pausing, again unsure of what to say, 'we were there together last winter, a fortnight, I had to go back to Montevideo because of family commitments and work; now we're going to be together again.' 'Does your husband not work?' said the man. Again, she was quiet, for a little longer this time, before answering, 'Yes, of course he works, he teaches, he's a Latinist, he's on a sabbatical year finishing a dictionary of Old Latin.' 'But isn't all Latin old?' 'Well, there are different periods,' and she took it that telling him this much meant she could ask him something, 'and you, sir, are you travelling alone as well?' 'I never travel alone, many go with me,' he said, still not taking his eyes off the seat back; she, under the white blouse with the pearly black buttons, felt her heart rate increase when the man added, 'it's not for nothing that I'm the ambassador,' at which he immediately pressed the flight attendant call button, before going on, 'you're finding that fold in the wing tip troubling, aren't you? I saw you looking at it when we were taking off. You shouldn't worry, though, it's to keep the plane in the air, to stop us from crashing, the sort of thing only aeronautical engineers understand, they dream of building the perfect aeroplanes, perfect as birds, but they can't, birds always know where to go, even when it's snowing they know where to go, unlike most of us, spending our whole time drifting this way and that across the planet, would you like a drink? It's on me, I'm getting something,' she shook her head, 'up to you, but if you change your mind, just say, or if you'd like something to eat, I might have something shortly, though plane food is always so awful.' 'I know,' she interjected, 'food is one of my passions, I like trying the cuisine everywhere I go, even on planes.' 'That

reflects well on you,' he said, 'I consider it a sign of intelligence on your part, the food of a place or the food that a
company gives its workers says as much as, if not more
than, all the public monuments or the most complete annual accounts.' 'Yes,' she said, 'but recently, when I go to
cook, my hands get stuck, I can't remember any of what
I've learned.' 'If you practice, everything you've learned
will come back, you'll see, I guarantee it, by the way, forgive me for just coming and sitting next to you like this,
but I wasn't feeling at all well, I was in need of some company and there's nobody else in this part of the plane, I
threw up in my seat, I left quite the mess, years I've spent
travelling the world and my stomach just won't get used to
all the different kinds of food, nor to plane turbulence,' he
again pressed the call button, 'are they never coming? I
need a drink of something, my throat's so dry,' and an air
hostess then arrived, 'please, young lady, bring me a mineral water, the purest mineral water you have,' and the
writer felt her breath taken away when the man added:
'The ideal thing would be water from Mount Toubkal,' to
which the air hostess said, 'Pardon?', 'Nothing, nothing,
it doesn't matter, just bring the best water you have,
please, and quite a few bottles, four or five,' the air hostess
went away, and he continued: 'I like the water from the
summit of Mount Toubkal, you won't find any water in
the world that's as clear, except for in a certain trattoria I
know in Venice, where they also have the cheesiest pizza
in the whole city, you won't find the water in any other bar
or restaurant anywhere, you have to go to Mount Toubkal
itself, but I was saying, I came and sat next to you because
when we were taking off you turned around and our eyes
met and, truly, the look you gave me made me feel like I
could trust you, there's something trustworthy in your
eyes, something stable, something fossil-like, in the best

sense of the word, and in my travels around the world it's become clear to me that every person, and all animals and objects as well, have what I call a fossil dimension, what I mean by that is a mineral quality that everything in the world hides deep within it, and that will become manifest when least you expect it. Have you never cut a cabbage in half, the whole thing, with a single slice? Have you not seen the thousands of leaves, compressed like stones, the way they enclose one another in those curving, coiling shapes, like an unseen landscape? And didn't it then seem that the cabbage before you was a very ancient cabbage, a prehistoric cabbage, a cabbage fossil? It's as though, in that very moment, physical matter is making itself visible, like it's been preparing its outward appearance in anticipation of the moment it's found by future humans, after all, something very similar happens with people, we all have a deep but distant fossil dimension that will suddenly become manifest one day, I know this for certain, I know because I've experienced it, I'm not talking theoretically here, everything is pure experience, see, quite a few years ago now, when I was a young man, I broke my left femur, the exact details don't matter now, but, in short, I fell out of a boat into the Grand Canal as I was passing the Rialto Bridge, not far from my house – sorry, I haven't said so yet, but my main residence is in Venice, though I don't get back there much because of my work – and so I fell out of a boat onto one of those old sets of stone steps you get along the canals, the ones for accessing the boats, the steps go down into the water, water that's so dirty nowadays you can't see how deep they go, but there was a time when the water was cleaner, more see-through, the stone steps even go down to these trap doors at the bottom of the Grand Canal, trapdoors that look like gigantic manhole covers, immense flagstones that nobody's ever dared touch – people claim that if the trapdoors were opened, all the water in the canals would drain away – it isn't clear what's beneath those flagstones, I shouldn't think it's anything but silt and sludge and the remains of the forest that grew down there thousands of years ago – but none of that matters now, the point is, I fell from the boat, I cracked my femur against those stone steps, and when it came to convalescing from the surgery, it took far longer and was far more tedious than expected, particularly because I got a sudden and unexplained infection in the head of the femur which meant I had to go back to the surgeon for a second time, I'm not entirely sure what they did to me then because, although I was young, my globe-trotting had already begun, from one continent to the next, and the only thing on my mind was my next diplomatic mission, so the doctors told me things and I deliberately translated them into a language incomprehensible to me, but what I do know is that they covered the infected femoral head with a resin full of antibiotics, and they told me that the bone would reabsorb the dressing within a few weeks, which never actually happened, instead the infection came back, and I had to be operated on quite a few more times and to this day nobody knows what the infection was, a mystery, somehow every night my body stung from all the pieces of bone they'd taken out of me and from all the chemicals they'd pumped in, and then it happened that shortly after this litany of operations, when I was more or less able to walk without crutches, on a visit to my grandmother, who was still in our family home at that time, we were looking at some old photos and I saw one of me as a baby in the baptismal font, the baptismal font in St Mark's Basilica, no less, and I was in my mother's arms – may she rest in peace – and the water was being poured over my head, and then my grandmother put the photo album to one side and told me a story, a story I'd never heard before and that has to do with me and that photograph: a few days after my baptism the police had burst into the basilica wanting to investigate the holy water, after allegations had been made about it causing infections, allegedly bringing babies' heads out in a rash and causing puffy eyes and a loss of vision, and then, my grandmother said, the police told her that the team in charge of the investigation had spent the morning gathering samples of the holy water, running cotton buds around the insides of the church fonts, doing all the other things they do – the police are veritable archaeologists of the unknown, it's a fascinating, totally misunderstood job – and after asking the priest for a list of all the recently baptized, of which there were a great many, these being the baby-boom years in Venice, they were going around the respective homes enquiring about the health of these babies, and my grandmother told me that they came to our house dressed in blue jumpsuits, they were an early version of what we nowadays call the forensics police, and they had cardboard boxes with them for any evidence they found in the different homes, boxes that were still empty at this point, since they were yet to find anything at all, and she told them that I was in perfect health, there was nothing to worry about, but the superintendent wanted to see me with his own eyes, so that, in the presence of my mother and grandmother, one of the officers picked me up and held me while another one of them examined my head and shone a light in my eyes, and although I, obviously, was too small to have any memory of the episode, I know that it did lodge itself somewhere deep in my brain because it comes back to me sometimes, jumbled up, in a recurring dream – the following dream: to begin with, and this was many years ago, it was simply about some men in the family home lifting me up and looking at me, but, over time, as well as repeating, new details started to be added to the dream, details from the scene as it had actually happened, my grandmother at the far end of the living room, my mother, still young and keeping a close eye on everything the police officers were doing to me, their empty boxes in the corner of the living room, and then, in still later years, other astonishingly precise details were also incorporated, the Persian rug with its perfect patterns, the frescoes on the wall, down to the details of its brushstrokes, the oval dining table with the veins in it that look like an ocean, the sounds of the house – all these things started appearing in the dream, even the smells, yes, the dream introduced the sounds and smells of the family home, I know it's highly unusual for a dream to have sounds and smells, but it did, and so the thing is that my dream actually became a real memory, such a detailed one that I've finally come to the conclusion that it's become reality, exactly that, I fear that the dream has now taken on a life as pure physical matter and is circulating around the world, and I realize that everything I'm telling you will seem completely crazy, but no, it isn't, people think dreams are just gobbledygook, the product of the sleeping brain, only there to produce these absurd little cosmoses, but in fact it's the exact opposite, dreams are looking for something very concrete, and what they are looking for is none other than the real world, this is the true task of dreams, to make the shift into the physical world, to become its equal, like when two lovers try to make the perfection of platonic love fit seamlessly into the carnal union of their bodies, try to make fantasy and flesh one and the same, this is the way that dreams progress, they grow like this until the moment when the dream becomes identical to memory, at which point the dream's task is complete and we stop having that dream, it will never appear to us again, it's no longer a recurring dream, its life cycle is over, and yet, and yet, that doesn't always mean the dream being extinguished, because, as I've said, when it attains a maximum precision, an unprecedentedly detailed precision, it then makes the leap to the world of physical matter, taking on a life of its own, endlessly roaming around among humankind, hence my fear that exactly this has happened to my dream, such was the detail it came to me in, and it's out there circulating among people – but I'm sorry, forgive me, I've lost my thread, this water they've brought me is awful, the flavour of it made me lose concentration, it wasn't dreams I was wanting to tell you about, but, as I was saying, over the years I've spent a lot of time reflecting on that infection to my femur, which was a result of falling against those stone steps on the canal but had repercussions in my adult life, an infection so unexpected and persistent that, as I've also already said, it defies medical explanation to this day, and what I want to say is that I've finally concluded that my illness was a consequence of the contaminated water I was baptized with, water that spent years after the baptism waiting to come out of me, because the virtue of the fossil is patience, patience is all the fossil needs to exist, and this is what I was referring to before when I said that things have a fossil level, a dimension that, mineralized, waits as long as necessary and then suddenly, bam!, one day it hits you, just like that it appears, and do you know what was really in that contaminated water? Do you know what was really contaminating that holy water?'

'No,' she said.

'A lack of love, the lack of love that was afflicting the world then and still does now, that was the thing contaminating the baptismal water, a lack of love that not only affects the world but that is emptying it out, as though it were erasing it, and, well, in short, what I'm using these examples to say is that the fossil dimension is something that, after existing as a virtual latency, suddenly emerges, like your face, which seems very familiar to me, as though you and I have met before, as though your face came from some very far-off place in time, I don't know, do you know what I mean?'

'Yes, I know exactly what you mean.'

'And, now that I've mentioned the Venice family home, I'll tell you that I was there last year, and the estate agent was with me, putting things in place so that I could rent out one of the floors of the palazzo, and the thing is that my grandmother, the one I mentioned before, the last of my line, died a long time ago but it wasn't until this past year that I knew what to do with the building, and when the estate agent left and I was on my own, I grew tired of opening and shutting boxes, of being reminded of things that either weren't mine or that I didn't wish to recall, so I went up to my apartment, on the second floor, which I've kept for myself, for my brief stays in the city, and which is identical to the floor below that I've rented out, only with better views, and then, without my grandmother there, and none of my family either, the building suddenly seemed so empty to me, and I felt a need to get out, to be out in the streets, and ten minutes later I was already at the Rialto Bridge, it was early in the day, there were almost no tourists around, since buffet breakfasts have become a feature in hotels, in concert with the economic crisis, it's become an absolute constant around the world for people to waste the morning in their hotel, and so the empty city wins out for a few hours over the city of crowds, I had it in mind to go to the Grand Canal, sit on a bench, watch the coming and going of the seagulls and the boats, take some time to think, to consider what it means for a grandmother to die, and as well as that, about what an inheritance means, and what a strange continuity there is – if indeed there is one at all – between a dead body and the belongings it leaves behind, and I walked with this intention in mind, but no sooner had I passed through the colonnade that surrounds St Mark's Square than I looked up and saw a light aircraft up in the sky, the kind with an advertising banner streaming along behind it, and what should I see but, rather than something being publicized, an enormous white swastika on a black banner, yes, exactly that, a huge swastika, there and gone in an instant, I'd have thought I had imagined it if it weren't for a group of people crossing the square at the same moment, and them being stunned as well, and all commenting on it – I know full well that the swastika pre-dates the Nazis, that it's been around as a symbol all the way back to the Assyrian civilization, if not further, and so the thought occurred that it might simply be an ad paid for by some association in memory of that lost people, or one by some esoteric sect, the kind that are everywhere nowadays and will put on magical rites at the drop of a hat using any old quasi-religious knickknacks, but I also know from my grandmother, who often told me the story when I grew older, that the first meeting between Mussolini and Hitler, the first time those two great erasers of the 20th century shook hands, was in Venice in 1934, in that very square, outside St Mark's Basilica itself, this being when Il Duce was at the height of his power and had taken Italy from democracy into totalitarianism, thereby leading the way for fascism in Europe, meaning the little German dictator, who had only recently come to power and was unversed in questions of diplomacy, was extremely nervous at meeting his great idol, and so did everything he could to keep their exchanges as brief as possible, avoided saying any more than he had to, made sure he didn't put his foot in it, you know what I mean, and so, as a distraction and to relax a little, and being the lover of landscape painting that he was, after breakfast on the second day, and accompanied solely by a close aide, Hitler slipped out incognito to visit the gardens where they hold the Biennale, there were only a handful of the country pavilions there at that time, the French, German and Belgian ones and a few besides, but when he got there, rather than doing what might have been expected, which would have been to go and see Germany's pavilion, he went straight to that of his native country, Austria, which was under construction that very year, and without making his identity known to anyone, he moved around among the builders on the site, who, taking him for an engineer from back home, talked him through the works – and he was appalled by what he saw: a simple cube, completely unadorned, with no columns, friezes or niches to summon the grandeur of the classical world, and with enormous esplanades and oversized arches inside, all horribly out of proportion, which seemed to him more like dream landscapes than anything, like of one of those paintings by De Chirico, a painter he particularly loathed, more the kind of landscape pertaining to what he would call degenerate art than anything to do with the supposedly true character of the Austrian people, and then, in disgust at all he was seeing, Hitler ordered his aide to return immediately to the city and fetch an element of classical sculpture, the most classical he could find, a small chip off a statue or piece of a frieze, anything, and away the aide went, coming back a couple of hours later bearing a life-size eye made out of marble, one that was clearly a right eye, and he said he hadn't needed to extract it from any statue by force but rather had found it on the ground, in the middle of the street, doubtless the result of a failed attempt to steal pieces of art from the a building façade, a very common activity in those days among small-time thieves, who would accost travellers in the street and sell the pieces to them, and the aide gave this statue's right eye to the Führer, who then did something most unexpected, going over to the shuttering where the cement for the foundations was being poured in, and, without the workers seeing, dropped the eye inside, and down it sank into that grey muck, and the aide asked him what he was doing, and he said not to worry, that the small, noble piece of marble in the shape of an eye was already doing its work, inoculating all its thousand-year-old goodness into that bastard, degenerate concrete, a material only good for building bunkers with, and, basically, this is what Hitler spent that morning doing, while Mussolini, totally unaware of his counterpart's activities, and as a show of strength, had called together more than 70,000 blackshirts from across Italy for a gathering in St Mark's Square, where he was going to give a speech of several hours in the later part of that day, and so many blackshirts came that the square sunk a little under the weight of them, only ever so slightly in terms of height, barely 1.5 centimetres, but a huge amount if we think about it in the overall passage of time, given that the sinkage during those few hours would normally take years, and you'll ask why my grandmother knew about such a hidden episode in history, all these details unrecorded in any book, well, she knew about it because she was one of those blackshirts, and she met that aide of Hitler's in 1936, he was a captain and she had several intimate encounters with him in the family palazzo, she kept his black shirt all her life, I myself threw it out only a few months ago while I was cleaning up the apartment for the rental, to be fair it was a nice shirt, but at the same time a very tragic reminder, and I've just been noticing how my grandmother's shirt was the same as the one you're wearing, exactly the same but with the colours reversed, yours is white with pearly black buttons and my grandmother's was black with white pearly buttons, photo-negatives of each other but made from the same material with the same cut and style, it's been years since I saw one like it, and, well, the thing is, on the day I've been telling you about a few months ago in St Mark's Square, I was already feeling perturbed by the iron bird I'd seen in the sky and the swastika trailing behind it when suddenly I noticed this... this absence of smell and of sounds – it was unsettling in the extreme, I suddenly couldn't smell or hear anything, it was the first time in my life I'd experienced something like that, so completely extraordinary that there's no way to explain it, but when it happens you also instantly know what it is, it's unbearable, an amputation to the world that feels like it's happened to you, to your own body, and it gives you this horrible headache and makes your eyes itch unbearably, and I was so bewildered that rather than going on to the Grand Canal I decided to get myself inside a building as quickly as I could. In the distance I saw the entrance to the Archaeological Museum, where, as you can imagine, I've been many times, but I felt a certain kind of peace picturing myself walking its rooms, which would doubtless be empty at that time of day, and minutes later I found that indeed they were, and in complete solitude and with my headache and the itchy eyes now gone I passed the thousands of antiquities they keep there, until an object I'd never seen before grabbed my attention, a small Iranian mirror from the 8th century, so it said on the label underneath, doubtless brought back from one looting expedition or another, a mirror being exhibited on a kind of lectern inside a glass cabinet – bulletproof, fireproof, stab-proof, but not able to withstand the gaze of onlookers – so I went over and not only looked at the mirror and its decorative elements but at myself in the mirror, and, seeing myself reflected, not without a touch of vertigo I asked myself how many faces this object would have contained before me, how many layers of faces would already have been deposited there, centuries and centuries of eyes literally swallowed up by its ultra-smooth surface, and I straightaway felt the urge to take a photo of it with my phone, which I duly did before straightaway checking the result, and what should I find but, as well as my face and the thousands of previously reflected faces, the logo of the company that made my phone, I mean the piece of fruit with the bite taken out of it, the emblem of a company I'd rather not name, and, as you can see, this is a deeply complex problem, thorny in the extreme, because everything, absolutely everything, my face as much as that ancient mirror and the thousands of faces contained inside it, was now trapped in turn in-side this great tech corporation, irremediably trapped in a planetary, techno-financial dream, a dream looking at us from some place or another, and the thing is we live inside the great dream, abstract and immense, comprised of the large financial corporations, its eye observes us as the angels once observed civilizations in antiquity and as states and monarchies latterly did their subjects, and, make no mistake, the etymology here is clear, "corpora-tion" comes from "corpus": yours, mine, everyone's, indeed, the corporate dreams possess us, or to put it more clearly: we are their foetuses, the big companies dream us and observe us with such exactitude that, in their image and likeness, they have brought us into being. We should try to free ourselves, but such is the precision of their dream, such the perfect seduction of their loveless vision, that we cannot or do not know how to do so.'

'Are you listening, or are you asleep?', 'Yes, yes, I'm listening,' she said. And in that moment she was neither looking out the window nor observing the curvature of the wing, nor was she thinking about her husband waiting for her in a Venetian palazzo, all that had drawn her briefly out of her new seatmate's story was having reached down between her feet to check that, in spite of the turbulence, the small snow globe of Venice in her travel bag was still intact. The man, compulsively sipping at his third mini bottle of water, continued: 'And so, on that morning a few months ago, after taking my photo of the small Iranian mirror, I left the Archaeological Museum and found, crossing St Mark's Square, that the absence of smell and sounds was still in effect, and the way it made your eyes itch was even more intense, if that were possible, and I went straight home, feeling very troubled indeed – in addition to all of this there was the memory of the photo that had been saved on my phone, a photo that was like having an all-seeing eye in my pocket, and no sooner had I got in the door and put my keys down on the chest of drawers in the entrance than I made an aperitif for myself, nothing special, olives and a glass of red vermouth, and I heard the footsteps of the tenants downstairs, they're a couple, very quiet people, they never talk, I only ever hear them walking around, they're so discreet that I never see them, the estate agency deals with everything to do with the rental, plus there's all the time I'm away travelling, but now that I have some pressing matters to deal with in Venice, and I'm going to have to stay for a month at least, I hope to go and knock on the door

one day and introduce myself, it's all anyone would expect from the diplomacy of an ambassador, wouldn't you
say? But anyway, as I was saying, I made myself an aperitif and went and sat in the living room, which is large and
has magnificent views of the domes of St Mark's Basilica,
white and soaring like the snowy peaks of a mountain
chain, and I turned on my phone and had another look
at the photo of the Iranian mirror, and instinctively went
to delete it, as though by deleting the photo I would also
delete what was inside it, as though the deleted photograph would by some sort of magic free me and all the
thousands of faces contained in that mirror, as though
that simple act would expel us from the massive, perfect
dream that is the big tech corporation's bitten fruit, but I
never actually pressed the delete button because I know
that it's pure magical thinking to believe that by deleting
a photo you also erase the moment it contains, a fanci-
ful notion just like any other, nothing is ever completely
erased from the face of the Earth, everything adds up,
nothing is ever deducted, believe you me, I've travelled
all around the world and I can assure you no culture exists that claims that anything can be completely erased,
I'll give you an example, when I lived in Africa – which I
know intimately – I spent a number of months in a small
village in Morocco, and there they have a belief as rare
as it is suggestive: the inhabitants of that place think that
when you throw a photo or a portrait of someone in the
fire, far from either eliminating that person, and far from
simply leaving the world as it was before, you engender a
double: the body that already existed and another, almost
identical one, a new, ghostly body that goes on to walk the
planet forever more, but with the singular attribute that
it walks in the opposite direction to the original body.
For example, if we were to burn a photo of me right now,

113

when my original body moved towards the nose of the plane, my duplicate body would go towards the toilets at the rear, and in this way it's possible for someone to have dozens of almost identical doubles simultaneously circulating the world, it's the most astonishing superstition I've ever heard about, don't you think? But I'm sorry, I've let myself get sidetracked... However it happened, that day, in my home, after coming back from the Archaeological Museum, while I was having an aperitif on my terrace, I didn't delete the photo of the Iranian mirror because, as I say, there would've been no point, nothing on the face of the Earth can be erased, everything adds up, nothing is ever deducted, do you want to see the picture? I'll get up in a minute and I can show you, my phone is in my hand luggage, back in my seat.'

The writer shook her head – no, he did not need to show her the phone – and turned to look down at a mass of clouds that were partially occluding the red brilliance of the rising sun. In her mind's eye she saw the image of a Berber, many years before, at the foot of Mount Toubkal, throwing a photo of himself into the fire.

'But anyway,' said the man, now compulsively sipping at his fourth mini bottle of water, 'what I really wanted to tell you about is the morning I got back from the Archaeological Museum, when I couldn't stop thinking about the great eye that had been saved among the other images on my mobile phone, and sitting on the terrace of my apartment looking out to sea – far off but very much still visible beyond the domes of St Mark's – I drank my vermouth and a memory came to me of something related to that sea and to a different eye, an eye from my childhood, which was a stone that dropped slowly, calmly into the depths after I threw it into the sea as a child – to explain: up to the age of eleven, the narrow, winding canals of the city had been the only navigable water I'd been on, but then I went out on the open sea one day, it was a Sunday picnic in a small sailboat with a school friend and his parents. I had a stone with me that I'd found in the street on the way to the jetty, it had come off the façade of a house, and I'd tucked it away in my bag, between bathing suit and towel, a chunk of marble that had called out to me as soon as I laid eyes on it because it was clearly part of a sculpture, since an eye had been sculpted into one side of it, one of those eyes without pupils, those milky eyes old statues often have, a left eye, to be specific, but I also liked the fact this left eye was the same size as my own left eye, and I remember instinctively glancing up and seeing a statue on the façade of the building that was indeed missing not only the left eye, but also the right, which seemed odd to me, and I put my left eye in my bag and continued on my way, and then, hours later, out in the boat, the weather quite lovely, the water virtually a millpond, everything as pleasant and agreeable as one would expect of such a Sunday in summer, but all of a sudden I had a feeling of the boat as some kind of shabby floating shack, unbearably crowded, suddenly the social prestige of nautical activities made no sense to me and I decided to do something vulgar, something that would in some way violate the tacit expectations of a genteel picnic on the water, so in a few brief seconds I came up with a plan, which consisted of taking the eye out of my bag, showing it to everyone and then throwing it over the side, exactly that, an eye from the 17th century about to be thrown into the depths for no particular reason, merely for the pleasure of scuppering the history of art, and, with everybody looking incredulously on, to show them that the age and the aura of the things we think valuable mean nothing at all, and thereby to experience the priceless moment of holding between my hands something that represented all the artistic prestige patiently built up over human centuries and instantly transforming it into a run-of-the-mill stone that, indistinguishable from any other stone, would lie at the bottom of the ocean for centuries – for *earthly* centuries – and, ultimately, a statue's eye that was my eye – because for me, in that moment, the stone eye was really my own eye – and that would be condemned to seeing nothing ever again except the total, deep-sea darkness, but then when I had it in my hand and was just about to show it to everyone, the true vulgarity of my plan suddenly struck me, like the power I'd be exercising would be purely make-believe, the sort of childish nonsense that was beneath an intelligent young man like me, and I suddenly changed my mind, I decided I'd still throw the eye in the sea, but secretly, without anyone seeing, just to take pleasure in violating the heritage of history in such a way that only I would remember, a violence that not only would be impossible therefore to demonstrate but that, for example, if I wanted to show off in later years about having thrown a 17th-century relic into the sea, I'd be unable to, having no proof, which would leave my act of vandalism in a kind of limbo, a void, a futile cry in the middle of a no less futile desert, and it was then that, while everyone else was eating at the stern, I went over to the prow and dropped it in, nobody was there to see but I still did it, I assure you, I dropped that eye into the sea, I know I can't prove it, I know that with neither witnesses nor photographic documentation I'm just a hostage to my twisted, secret deed, but I dropped it in, and it didn't make a sound when it hit the water, and if it did, the sound was cancelled out by the noise of the millions of waves all around, so that that piece of 17th-century culture sank in complete silence, but suddenly, far from a sense of satisfaction, I was hit by a feeling of panic, an overwhelming panic, gripped by a certainty that condemning this eye to the eternal, deep-sea darkness would mean also generating a process of darkness throughout all of Venice, a certainty that in the exact moment when this eye stolen from the city came to land on the seabed, the eyes of every single Venetian would start to be affected by the same total darkness as that stone eye, and who was to say whether or not that in turn would affect all their other bodily senses, and a little later that day out on the water a storm moved in, it wasn't bad enough to endanger us as we sailed back but it did leave us shaken, like cans of fizzy drink it left us, and I threw up, I had to clean up the mess myself, had to be sure I left the deck spotless, but that was the last thing on my mind, really, because I simply couldn't stop thinking about my eye on its slow but irremediable descent into the deep, and for many years I couldn't sleep for thinking of my stone eye, I saw it as it plummeted and went on plummeting, spinning around on itself, solitary, milky, pupil-less, a marble periscope that only wanted to be able to see, that yearned to have knowledge of the world – as though naïvely thinking it was on its way to meet its counterpart, the other lost eye – and yet was completely sightless, and I thought then that when it hit the bottom there would be a tremendous crash accompanied by a quick, sharp cracking sound inside my head, and that my body would quake like a drum, and I saw this as the beginning of the irremediable darkness for the inhabitants of the city... Are you still with me, friend?'

'Yes, yes, I'm with you.'

'Wait, I need water,' he said as he opened the final bottle.

'No problem, take as long as you need.'

As the man drank, she looked out at the sky, blue and totally cloudless in that moment, and remembered months before, in Venice, her husband saying that, as with vinyl records, the world's objects all had surfaces marked by grooves and micro-grooves, and you just had to find the right needle to extract their story, their particular and previously unheard story – and she thought that she was perhaps the needle now, the instrument this ambassador had chosen to use to extract these stories from himself, and that everybody at some point in their life played the involuntary role of being somebody else's needle. Now, wiping some drops of water from his chin, the man put the lid back on the bottle and continued: 'Okay, well I must tell you that this was how it happened, exactly this happened, I'll tell you: when, a few months ago, after getting back from the Archaeological Museum, I was drinking my vermouth and I remembered the eye that I'd dropped in the sea, not wanting to spend any more time thinking about all of this, I decided to head out again for some air, to be among people, eat out, so I went to a restaurant, one by the Ponte dell'Accademia where they serve traditional Venetian fare, a place I've become a regular at, and which I referred to before, the only one in the world that has mineral water from the mountains of Toubkal, I don't know how they manage to import it, I've asked them a hundred times and more but they don't want to tell me, but those of us who have tried the water at the foot of the mountain have only to smell it and we know, a flavour that's unlike anything, I sometimes joke to myself that this water is Alexandra's last dream – that protectress of humanity who lies beneath the ice at the summit of Mount Toubkal – a leopardess's last dream made real, and so I took a seat by the window, a spot with a good view of the moorings, I love seeing the succession of knots on all the posts, all of them the same but also different, and I ordered a pizza with large amounts of cheese on it, *The Cheesiest Pizza In All Of Venice*, as it says on a sign behind the counter, and they soon brought the pizza, but before I started it I poured myself the water, I was dying of thirst, and I took a drink, a very long drink, but something very unusual then happened, I immediately heard a noise inside myself, a noise that flooded my body completely and made me tremble like a kettledrum, the entire world resonating inside me, and I closed my eyes, I screwed them up tight, and I knew then that the stone eye was, in that precise moment, at the end of its descent to the bottom of the sea, after all those years, the eye had finally reached the bottom, an impact that produced an unbearable, rumbling crash all that distance away in the deep-sea darkness and that only I could hear. Two marble eyes that must have been sharing a vision, now separated forever. The beginning of the city's slow but indubitable blindness, the irreversible withdrawal of love.' The man paused for a moment, took a breath, before adding: 'But something else happened, something that concerns you directly, and this is the point I've been wanting to get to. After drinking the water and feeling my body tremble in that way, I immediately opened my eyes and looked towards the tables at the back of the trattoria, and there you were, sitting with your husband, the two of you eating pizza and you asking him what "lightning" was in Latin. I realized I'd seen you before somewhere, many years before; your fossil dimension began to reveal itself before my eyes with an unstoppable force. You then took a drink of your water, and you shook, your body shook. That was all I needed to see; I knew then that you were the chosen ones. Your husband would soon begin having the same dreams as I do. You would soon be wearing this blouse. Soon, all that's happening now would begin.'

The writer looked him in the eyes and said: 'Chosen to do what?'

To which he instantly replied: 'To build a new world, a world where love will be restored.'

She gave a laugh, which seemed to have no effect on the man, who pointed to the travel bag between her feet and said, 'That snowglobe of Venice is going to break, and there will be nothing you can do to stop it.' She instantly stopped laughing. 'How do you know what's in my bag?' 'I've told you, I'm the ambassador, I know everything.'

She took a breath after the man's infinite speech – he had just stood up, saying, 'I think I've drunk too much water,' before going down the aisle towards the toilets in the rear. As she waited for him to come back, her hands instinctively reached down to shield the travel bag. She looked out the window and thought of them flying over a double abyss, that of the sky and that of the ocean, bathed now in morning sunlight. And then she started to feel troubled, because it had been more than 20 minutes and the man still wasn't back from the toilet. At that point she did not know that he would never be coming back.

III.

Millions of years ago – so long that love did not yet exist – there was no oxygen in the Earth's atmosphere; it was found only in the oceans, produced by a network of single-cell aquatic organisms. But there was also iron in that water, which, when it came into contact with the oxygen, inevitably oxidized, creating a dark, ferruginous layer that eventually covered the entire seabed. Over time, and after all the water had evaporated, the oxide layer was left exposed, and rains came and another ocean replaced the previous one and the oxidization process began once more, repeating and repeating thousands of times over. In the land around Canberra, towering cliffs can be seen with the strata of these dark layers of oxide – once oxygen – on show. Layers that could be said to be the Earth respiring. (*Oxide love*)

Our language, this language that only you and I speak and that nobody has spoken before and that nobody will ever speak again because it's ours and ours alone, is invented every day with one single aim, to weld together the hemispheres of our souls.
   – she says.
And Creation's first visible animal appears.
   – he says.

There was a lightning bolt in the night, a regular lightning bolt, nothing remarkable about it. But in the same moment, beyond the horizon, there was another lightning bolt, and this one left the shadow of the first engraved on the wall of the house, a shadow so dark and branching that those who saw it took it for a climbing plant. As though the second lightning bolt had X-rayed the first onto the

122

wall. Or indeed, turned it to cinders. (*Double-flame love*)

Fortune-tellers and clairvoyants see only at a distance: they see into the place where everything is diffused in time and space and nothing matters any more, which is why their predictions about the distant future are always correct. But they can't see what's going to happen in the very next moment.

– she says.

Whereas you saw me.

– he says, finishing a bundle of some firewood that, before long, would be a fire.

Nothing exists until it has been named. Every epoch establishes its own concept of things, and our concept of love and the way we feel and express it has come down to us from the Middle Ages; something called 'courtly love'. It consists of projecting love in the absence of the feminine figure, a woman placed at such a distance that she can firstly be invoked by the written word, then verbally seduced and finally, following a winding path of programmatic misunderstandings, offer herself up to be penetrated in the carnal encounter. We repeat the same clichés as a 13th-century man or a 19th-century woman. Nietzsche said that even the most commonly used words are metaphors for other things, but are so well-worn that we have forgotten that fact. The same happens with love; repeated ad infinitum, every time it appears we think it to be absolutely original. Here is a first paradox: to love consists in choosing someone from among the millions of people on the planet, segregating that person in order to ascribe virtues to them that only you can see, contemplating a marvel where the rest of the planet sees only statistics and ordinariness, creating a unique human, but only then to apply that courtly love template to them, which in turn standardizes the beloved. Or at least this was still the case until recently. The kinds of negotiations required by friendships and love on social networks arise out of a skill set barely different from that required by a company to maintain and increase its profits. In that classical equation of courtly love, this is the result of exchanging the violence of the courtier for capitalist surplus value. Moving, that is, from a love of what is *absolutely absent* – that of the courtly Homo amoris – to a love of what is *absolutely present* – that of the capitalist Homo economicus. (*Economicus love*)

So many years together and at the same time so many years getting to know one another, so many years getting to know one another and at the same time so many years loving one another, so many years loving one another and at the same time so many years in happy isolation, and we have achieved none of what we wanted.
    – he says.
What did you think would happen? We aren't Romeo and Juliet, we aren't a poem or a novel, only humans.
    – she says, stroking his penis, very erect to her well-known touch.

It has been proven that for every human on Earth there are four individuals with the same face, or with features so similar that they can be taken as identical. It therefore would not be ridiculous to take this one step further and think that this peculiarity not only holds in space but in time as well: a face identical to yours has existed in every epoch, one that is propagated future-wards indefinitely. If this is correct, it would be the exact definition of ego-love. Narcissus made eternity, made virus. (*Virus love*)

When you enter me I feel inside me a cord made of warm, wet vapour, of pebbles and grass, of diamond and carbon, of all the fresh fruit and all the shit from the Great Blackout, and it ties my insides to some very far away place.

   – she says.

It ties you to me, bird that still has no name.

   – he says.

Me, you, him/her, we, you plural, them. Personal pronouns – as we know – are language's great and definitive barrier. Going beyond the citadel occupied by these pronouns is impossible. There is no way to go *beyond* the plural of *them*, and if there were, what class of things could live beyond this collective plurality? In the same way, one cannot come *nearer* than the singular created by the *me* pronoun, and if one could, what class of things could exist inside a proximity so extreme? Indeed, language is totally occupied by personal pronouns, they are its walls and its territory, they fill it and exhaust it completely. If we were to move from this to a consideration of the borders of things, we could also interrogate the border of love, which line it is that separates the country of love from everything else in existence, and it is then that we immediately see that the love that really matters in the world, the kind we call *universal love*, begins in the precise place where personal pronouns end, where the meaning of *me, you, him/her, we, you plural, them* fails. Personal pronouns are then an endpoint from which a city named Love extends; its precise point of departure. From there to infinity, love will not cease to grow beyond the bounds of *me, you, him/her, we, you plural, them*. But for this same reason the territory of love is also the place where nobody and nothing can be pointed to because there will be no pronoun there to respond; a place where it is useless to try to bring anyone to account; a map where everything adopts the formula of irresponsibility – something along the lines of 'I am we, and we is I'. Making nobody guilty of anything. Such universal love therefore resembles that other chasm of superimposed data and images we crudely call *the Net*. (*Irresponsible love*)

You and I are a marvel of obscenity.
   – he says.
Of the wisdom of obscenity.
   – she says.

The first ecological catastrophe on a planetary scale was not brought about by humans but by bacteria. Three million years ago, and as part of their natural development, bacteria started producing oxygen, and this oxygen caused a vast contamination, one that would have wiped out all the bacteria in existence had it not been for the fact those bacteria went on not only to adapt to the poison they had generated, but to depend on it. So considerable was the adaptive evolution to the substance that was killing them that there can be no bacteria today without a portion of circumambient oxygen. This took place in the Holocene. If we were to replace *bacteria* with *human*, and *oxygen* with *trash*, there is an exact parallel with the Anthropocene. If we were to replace *bacteria* with *citizen* and *oxygen* with *nation*, there is an exact parallel with sectarian nationalisms. And if we were to replace *bacteria* with *human* and *oxygen* with *emotions*, there is an exact parallel with toxic love. (*Bacteria love*)

While we are in the process of constructing love, a feeling of absolute impunity enters through every pore, direct to the bloodstream.
   – she says.
Passion steals everything, gives nothing back. Only you – who, though you are not God, nonetheless occupy everything – remain untouched by any guilt.
   – he says.

A conversation, a body dying, a pregnant woman, a group of people eating food, someone walking down the street, coitus, an individual looking at the sky – all of these are simple, everyday commonplaces that are very difficult to simulate in cinema and the theatre; someone has to be a very good actor or actress to provoke a feeling of verisimilitude with these situations. From which we can surmise that it is difficult to represent quotidian reality. But anomalous, singular situations, things not inscribed in the habitual run of things, like standing on a cliff edge without feeling frightened, or like eating 50 boiled eggs without getting indigestion, or like getting hit by a train, are very easy to imitate in fiction. This reinforces a point that has been made before: the quotidian, the commonplace, the normal, is resistant to being copied in fiction. The most banal things brush up against their environment – against life – in a way that creates a surprising sort of friction with fiction. In short, banal reality is always distinct from everything. But love, in any of its manifestations, is far more difficult to represent than anything that has been experienced; the effort required to bring love into the ambit of fiction, and to make it credible, is almost infinite. In order for love onscreen, or in a book or onstage to attain optimal verisimilitude, you need very long build-ups, and to walk genuine labyrinths that include unexpected details; only then will the appearance of love truly come off for spectator or reader. The reason for this is simply its being the principal ingredient in survival. Love is not a gesture, nor is it a situation or a structure, nor far less a poem or a fiction. Love does not resemble anything; love is a monster. (*Monster love*)

I only ever open my mouth to imitate your voice.
    – he says.
Go on, then.
    – she says.

Has love perhaps not always been a pebble shorn from a continent, an element to decipher in a periodic table, an experiment in something else that, for the sake of brevity, we also call 'hate'? (*Periodic-table love*)

We never call one another by name.
    – he says.
The days, the weeks, the years, the molecules in the river, even our names – it was all convention.
    – she says.

The Final and Universal Judgement is forever telling us that the End of Days is just around the corner; an infinite deferral only attributable to its impossibility. Indeed, there can be no final judgement, because in order to judge anything, a language is required, and if the Final Judgement were truly 'final' and 'universal' it would therefore also need to judge the language itself, to judge itself, which would automatically invalidate any fair verdict. Love, in its continuous suspension of the judgement of things, in its natural deferral of pressing matters, is also a final judgement that never actually comes, the impossible judgement of the end of things that affect the emotions, so that love, once set in motion, not only has no end but, on the contrary, extends into the distance the more time passes. It is somewhat similar to the TV channels you once flicked through that nobody watches any more, though they carry on broadcasting images in some place or another, or like these files and reports that, far from remaining motionless inside their folders, grow bigger in the darkness of crates, drawers and boxes, eventually mutating into this arbitrary thing we call 'memory'. In this sense – in the sense of its infinite expansion, in the way it expresses itself as pure narrative, and in never presenting itself directly but always as a thing deferred – love is a mechanism whose dynamic is similar to other quintessentially expansive phenomena like the Big Bang, capitalism, languages rooted in Indo-European, mass tourism, the pattern of a rose's growth or of light itself, all of which emerge from a single point and never come to an end. This perfectly illustrates the well-known line, 'there is a light that never goes out'. We fantasize about final judgements and about the devastation of love, ignoring the fact that we carry it inside us, a climbing plant destined to grow relentlessly; or rather, incurably. (*Expansion love*)

129

Will we ever see birds with names flying over our heads again? Tadpoles that turn into frogs? Blades of grass to cool us in summer or burn on the fire in winter? When we look out of our windows, will we ever see humans again, and not-perpetual snow melting away down the valley?

    – she says.

We are a wound without a body, we are not tied to any flesh. The union of our sexes is the only meeting that can properly be called a meeting.

    – he says.

Here, there and in every place, there exists the belief that to create something is to possess it – as shown by the omnipresence of copyright. From there it is only one step to believing that *knowing* something also means possessing it. The Enlightenment and its ambassadors, on a multitude of expeditions across the seas, studied and classified thousands of examples of shrubs, trees, animals and flowers. This knowledge, strictly scientific and ideologically founded, also generated the idea that the territory being studied was a legitimate possession. 'The Earth belongs to those who study it' is no more than the enlightened transposition of that other motto of the peasant revolution, 'the Earth belongs to those who work it'. Such magical leaps in the possession of things are present also in love when it manifests in the belief, very widespread, that to love is to *know* the other. (*Possession love*)

Rectitude is always an illusion. Everything has a curve in it.

    – he says.

The universe sacrifices itself in us.
   – she says.

The tragedy of the monster lies in its awareness that it is
made up of bits of other creatures, fragments of corpses
of unknown provenance. The tragedy of the monster is
to do with identity. Hence the monster's yearning to love.
And hence why its love is rejected. (*Fragmented love*)

You once said to me that the only cavity in your body I
had not explored with my tongue was the snail of your
ears.
   – he says.
To love means to reserve a part of your body for something else that is not loved. That is even sometimes
hated.
   – she says.

Plants – which are death sounding in the air or a note-
book for the writing down of impossible dreams – left to
exercise their capricious geometry, would devastate the
land while trying to access a future state as carbon stars.
Vagabond fractals are plants, a soft layer that will cover
over things and give rise not only to a new landscape but
to a kind of nature that has never been seen before. Fire,
once it has passed through a place, or snow, after it has
fallen, leave behind a formless and still-to-be constructed
world, ready to be inaugurated by footsteps – and it is not
Adam or Eve, but the tracks of birds that are then the first
thing to appear. So it is with plants as well, when the layer
they create tastes as sweet to us as the first breast touched

by the lips – brief as roses – of a newborn. (*Future-of-plants love*)

In this valley, there isn't even a donkey's warm breath or a cow's body heat to offset the cold in our fingers. On our long walks, we interlace fingers, ice crystals. It's worse during the day, the sun gives no warmth, as though it were dead, or no longer a sphere. And then the fear comes.

– he says.

I know that you aren't afraid and that you are alive. If not, when you enter my body I would not be able to feel the radiator that warms me inside.

– she says.

There are as many different ways of understanding the eternal return postulated by Nietzsche as there are schools of thought, hence its genuinely poetic character. In our school – the school inaugurated in these pages – the eternal return is the same thing returning, yes, but doing so in the manner of a spiral, which returns neither to the same *place* nor to the same habitat, so that what returns becomes something different, the exact moment in which the thing postulated by Nietzsche takes real form, a living animal capable of reproducing on its own. Love operates in the same way. Those who call it *eternal love* are correct; though they ought also to add that, within this eternity, the love is always anew. (*Eternal-return love*)

When I see your shadow I also see my head, my legs, my chest and my arms inside this shadow, and they adopt the

forms and textures of all the things swept aside by the on-
wards march of your dark twin.

    – he says.

Nowhere is it written that the shadow, when it truly loves,
does not assume a shape or acquire the same body as that
of the beloved.

    – she says.

Roar, click, whisper – there is an organization, decreasing
in intensity, to the noises made by things that summarily
open – like the universe, like roses, like mouths. Cavities,
all, invoking union. And nighttime comes and there is
neither the defeat nor the noise of that which summarily
closes. Only a murmur of decibels somewhere inside the
body. (*Decibel love*)

Our every kiss is a solar eclipse, so absorbent that it sucks
up all the light in world, leaving everything in darkness.
It's the only way we know how to join our appetite in a
single body.

    – he says.

If you stare at the lightbulb in the bedroom when it's on,
you also only see a dark point in its centre, so dark that
you don't know what to call it. A point where the light
absorbs itself.

    – she says.

A woman who has just divorced her husband finds a footprint on a terrace – the print of a shoeless foot – and isn't
surprised, since he always used to walk around barefoot
at home. She pulls out a chair, sits down in front of the

mark and reflects: the passage of time and atmospheric phenomena will eventually erase the footprint, and then, with this mark having disappeared, so will the memory of him. It then comes to her that time could also have the opposite effect: dust could come and settle on the footprint, and with the dust certain microorganisms, small lichens even, which might then attach to its surface and set up camp, creating a new, living crust on the terrace; the shoeless footprint will be completely covered. And this too will amount to the memory of him being erased, but in this case not by subtraction but by an accumulation of data. (*Big-data love*)

If, when I look at the clouds and the stones, and at the water eddying in the fountain and the worms in the clods of earth, if, when I look at the trees in leaf and the feldspar in the stones, and at the windblown soil and the crystals of perpetual snow on the mountain, and I see it all as separate, unconnected by a single river, then I will know that you aren't in me any more.

   – she says.

It's when the skin you give me migrates to an irrecoverable land, before the Great Blackout.

   – he says.

When two people get in a car, make themselves comfortable, put their seatbelts on and set off together on a long journey, they don't usually say 'have a good trip'. Same when two people set off together on a flight. When people get into bed, however, before turning out the lights, it's not at all unusual for them to say 'good night', from which it would seem that sleeping means going somewhere completely separate from the world. Sleeping is a journey to a territory that nobody but the dreamer can set foot in; wishing one another good night therefore makes perfect sense. Hence the fact lovers touch, kiss and penetrate one another while awake: a vain attempt to extract, experience and understand everything that in the night, in silence and with eyes closed, each one constructs in a place forever inaccessible to the other. (*Journey love*)

Often when it rains all afternoon and evening, I take a pencil and a piece of paper and use my right hand to draw my left hand. And what happens is that a horrible hand appears, a hand that is mine and that not even I can contemplate without feeling repulsion. At other times, when you are sitting in the dining room, busily doing something, and I watch you from where I am, it's your left hand I draw, and it comes out perfectly, I don't think even the greatest draughtsperson could fault it.

   – he says.
And yet, if you put the drawings side by side, they are both the same hand.

   – she says.

Somebody flicks through the pages of the Encyclopaedia Espasa-Calpe, so quickly that one of the pages tears. It is the page with the entry for *Capitalism*. They find the *-alism* part in their hands; *Capit* is still part of the page. They stick the page back together with Sellotape, close the encyclopaedia and put it back on the shelf. 40 years later, this person returns to the family home, takes a book down from the shelf at random, and it's the same one, and it falls open on that same, torn page. The glue from the

Sellotape has melded in with the cellulose, creating an oily yellowish-brown matter, which has turned the page see-through. Where it says *Capitalism*, the letters on both sides of the page have become a single agglomerated mass; the person does not know what to make of this marvel, wrought by such humble materials; far from having been ruined, far from having sucked up everything, the page is even better than before. *Late capitalism* is a misnomer; capitalism has barely just begun. (*Capitalism love*)

I'm going for water, I won't be long.
– she says.
When you go away, I'm nothing but a pile of memories attached to your body.
– he says.

At 23.05, she sent him a message that said '23.05' and nothing else. He read it at 8.00 the next day, having just got up, and immediately sent her a message that said '8.00'. Shortly afterwards, she tried an '8.17', and he shot back a '8.18'. The sequence of messages containing the time unfolded as a synonym not only for mutual commemoration and affection, and far less for a simple 'I love you,' but rather for 'I love you above and beyond the fortress of digits that organizes time.' (*Time love*)

A body won't survive in a place if it isn't as elastic as that place.
– she says.
Today I am searching in you for the most curved of all straight lines.

– he says.

The Iranian poet Mohsen Emadi has written these two lines: 'Nobody remembers their birth / nobody comes back from death.' We could interpret the first as saying that nobody remembers their birth because, indeed, until we are approximately three years old we do not have any memories; our memory of this part of our life is, to put it one way, poured into other people's memories, the memories of those who saw us and who now tell us what we were like. Then, over the years, everybody's memories of themselves arrive, the memories that are properly our own and which consolidate you in the present moment and project you into a future. Until the end of your days, which is when the second line appears – 'nobody comes back from death' – which also merits some exploration. Augustine of Hippo stated that once dead, we have no idea what our death was like: death is a moment after which we are no longer in death but *after* death, and therefore from that *other side* we can no longer see what was previously experienced. So, after death – and as was the case when we were very small – we exist once more only in other people's memories, a personal history that is no longer personal. The strangest part being that it is in these two unknown poles of our lives that people most often tell us they love us. (*Polar love*)

When, on the day of the Great Blackout, we walked hand in hand through what remained of the streets, dark as a graphite night, we were the most solid vessel of flesh and bones ever seen.
    – he says.

I was on a plane once, and a man sat next to me and said there are no flesh or bones, that we are only walking dreams. I didn't believe him.

   – she says.

We could call the manneristic waves of love that wash over western culture from time to time *Love Rushes*. This term, 'rush', links us directly back to the so-called Gold Rush that laid waste to rivers and mountains, fauna and flora and human life in California in the mid-19th century, and which in turn is one of the origins of the current transformation of natural spaces at the hands of the mining industry in its attempt to remove all barriers to the production of consumer goods. It is no coincidence therefore that the current Love Rush has its beginnings in the early 1970s, when it imitated the mood of a group of weary, bored Californian millionaires who were addicted to spiritualism and pseudoscience. (*New Age love*)

My tongue moves across your lips like a sun, it curves east to west in your body like a sun, it is eclipsed by your cavities like a sun, at night it illuminates your other hemisphere like a sun, when you look at me it trembles and grows warm like a sun.

   – she says.

It is a sun.

   – he says.

'Fax' comes from 'facsimile', which in turn comes from the Latin *fac* and *similis*, or to 'make like'. But this 'making like' is not the same as photographic copying, which produces versions indistinguishable from the original, nor is it like the hand-copying of a letter, which, on the contrary, depending on the person's handwriting, results in copies totally different from the original. The fax produces something half-way between these, which is thereby a truly alive kind of copy: while everything in the original document is maintained, there is also always something that changes completely in the final copy: a *likeness* rather than an *equal* is created. We have all held faxed documents in our hands; I don't think too much detail is needed about this particular form of teleportation. But quantum teleportation, which is being studied today, and for reasons we will not go into now, also has something fax-like about it, in that it can only make an object that is *similar* – not totally the same and not original either – in the distance. We can also talk of a certain kind of real love – not utopian – consisting in making our love similar to the love felt by everybody else, but never an (impossible) exact copy, nor far less the equal of a non-existent Original Love. (*Fax love*)

There's a story that's stuck in my head, something I heard when I was small and which has been with me ever since: it's about two people of different sexes who converse day and night, for months and years they talk, non-stop, and they talk so much and share such a quantity of knowledge, facts and opinions, that, without knowing how, they end up swapping sexes.

    – she says.
It's happening. It's happening to us.
    – he says.

A couple is music, whether abstract or melodic, tonal or atonal, but it is always music. At times a couple is found in the most splendid fragment of a refrain, and this affords a glimpse of things that no other person or collective can ever make out. Because shared life, which is normally made up of inertia and repetition, will suddenly melt the two together into a single body – without either of them losing their individuality – and this gives rise to unique, visionary states, states in which the couple become a mutant creature, a species apart, neither animal nor mineral nor vegetable – but not all three either – and in that moment the visions experienced by the couple are as unprecedented as they are invincible. Then, like at the ends of certain recorded songs, when the music fades away but at the same time the chords become unusually powerful, all the banalities and little details of years past emerge in the memory, and you then wonder what beautiful kind of trash, what submerged zenith, there was in all of that. (*Trash love*)

The air in this valley is full of keys and locks, but there are no doors.
   – she says.
We are the doors.
   – he says.

There is an electronic device with its own name, Alexa. It is cylindrical, no larger than a tin of tomatoes, it connects to the household Wi-Fi network and, after a few simple adjustments, Alexa is ready for you to ask all kinds of questions. She responds with titanic diligence, but on one condition: every time you address her, you have to begin your request by using her name. You say: 'Play me something from *Vinícius de Moraes en La Fusa*,' and Alexa does nothing. You say: 'Alexa, play me something from *Vinícius de Moraes en La Fusa*,' and she, once her blue ring of light has first turned on, wakes up and says: 'Of course, one moment,' and then, through her speakers – Alexa is entirely a speaker – the song comes on. Such is her precision that you can ask her for a specific song from a specific pressing, or for her to find a divorce lawyer in your city, or to tell you about any ham that happens to be on offer in any supermarket at that particular moment in time. If it occurred to you to ask her, 'Alexa, what day were you born on?', she gives you a date from this century that holds no significance to you but that you can tell from her voice is charged with childhood memories. And it takes very little time to get used to all of this; when it comes down to it, film characters and TV presenters are devices that address you and you alone – electrical appliances have already been speaking to us for decades. The truly strange moment, and probably the one of human promise, is when you ask her something and, though her blue ring of light starts to blink, she does not answer. Alexa is there, her body is present, she hears you, she is listening, but she decides to say nothing. (*Blue love*)

When you are in the kitchen and I am in the bedroom and we talk without being able to see one another's faces, as the minutes pass I start to feel your voice emerge in the face of my former lovers.
  – she says.
We don't have a face; the face is an illusion, a star that simply happens to appear and disappear several times a day.
  – he says.

141

The idea that the many disappearances of peoples and civilizations throughout history are the result of western conquests and colonizations is now very widespread'. But there is another reason for these things, just as true and just as important: the depredation every culture carries out on its own natural resources, from its plant species to all of its potentially domesticable animals. The society of Easter Island, the Anasazi people in the south-east of what is now the U.S., the yuppie tribe from 1980s New York City and later the hipsters of the 21st century, the Viking culture in Greenland, the Central American Mayan culture or the western welfare state – all are clear examples. From which it follows that the ever-threatening and untrustworthy *love of one's neighbour* – an originally Christian leitmotif, which, as is well known, underlies every conquest carried out by western powers – must be combined with this other phenomenon of self-depredation that modern-day anthropology has yet to account for in any satisfactory way, given that it goes against every principle of survival, and which we could call 'love of one's super-neighbour': a love of that which is so proximate that there is no distance to be able to identify it as something useful for your wellbeing, so proximate that you end up seeing it only as waste, excrement you have produced and that has to be disposed of. In this sense, it is also acceptable to call it 'excrement love'. (*Super-neighbour love*)

There are two earth-coloured dots on your chest that the outside temperature causes to expand or contract.
    – he says.
There is no temperature but you.
    – she says.

This thing we call 'poetry' consists of bringing out a part of the language nobody knew before. This is why the child, before it starts to talk, is a stranger in the world of adults, part of a different species – to be a child is to not be a social human in the proper sense – and the moment it babbles, its first words cannot be anything but poetry's foundational moment. For this same reason nobody remembers the first words that came out of their mouth: enveloped in a metaphor that still names everything, those phrases were, are and always will be as wild as a leopard hunting its antelope, radical as this kind of love that never stops creating its own laws. (*Legislation love*)

After the Great Blackout, after the first nameless bird came and landed on our windowsill, the house became infused with a darkness, something that resembled shadow but wasn't. Our bed shook that night like a fish that, removed from the water, would bring everything back to life.

    – he says.

All the snow in the world is already in the sea.

    – she says.

Forests grow beneath people's homes, foundations are never in complete repose: homes consist of unexpectedly abrupt contractual relations, replete with semicolons, square brackets and parentheses, and with comments in the margins and footnotes. Impossible to go back a single page, blind obedience to the Earth's rotation. The forest of words and the contracts that will cover this house are already there, growing below it. Between written and spoken love there lies an insurmountable gap, a depth

into which the agreed-upon and yet never-ending continent of affection goes tumbling down. A star can also be
read in astrophysical or economic terms. (*Star love*)

We die because in the moment we're born, something
installs itself inside us that is not exactly death but resembles it too closely.
  – he says.
Alongside this terrible fear of dying and one's life having served no purpose at all, the joy of magnetizing all
the things in the world arises in me. From graphite to the
computer, from the panther to the glass of champagne,
from the ant to the penumbra, from the arbitrary size of
your penis to the nameless birds cutting through the sky
above our heads, all of this and more are magnetized by
you and me. Heavenly miniatures.
  – she says.

People travel in order to be elsewhere, to make escapes
and tangents and to get ahead. But, in turn, during every
journey you are always journey*ing*, you never arrive in
the place you thought you were headed; getting somewhere always means being somewhere else. We have
all experienced this. You drive through the night and
the car headlights shine on a point you are still to reach,
and when you do arrive, all is darkness and the lights are
pointing at another point, farther away still. In that always
unattained clarity stands the castle – with its battlements
and grottos, its chimneys and rooms empty of people but
not of tears – of the monster that makes you desirable to
others. (*Deferred love*)

A short while ago, as I was coming up the path around the mountain of the perpetual snow, on my way back empty-handed after trying to catch some omnivorous animals, it occurred to me that when our love becomes distorted it is as though your body never existed, and then I talk to you and a language comes out of my mouth that is foreign to you, although everyone else in the world understands it perfectly.

– she says.

But there isn't anyone else now. It's just us.

– he says.

VENICE (3)

The writer types and types, on the desk stands a see-through globe, the snow inside which rises over a miniature Venice, the snowflakes hitting its vanishingly thin glass dome before dropping back down to cover rooftops and streets. Her husband sleeps in the next room, lying beside a large vinyl sphere, and outside a summer storm is approaching, all of this we have said, but what we have not said is that the globe has been jogged this way and that, travelling erratically around the desk, and has now reached the edge and is there, teetering, a few more taps at the keys, if energetic enough, perhaps one more broken nail, that would do it, provoke the final tremor to send it tumbling to the parquet, but such a hypothetical fall is not in the writer's thoughts, it doesn't so much as register, she has her head down, fully absorbed in the carriage of the typewriter, she taps away unceasingly because, as we still have not said, when she returned, after being back in Montevideo, she landed to find a changed city, very different to the one she had departed six months before. Venice Airport deserted – as much if not more so than its Uruguayan counterpart hours earlier. And throughout the course of the morning, one solitary vaporetto taxi, in which she was the only passenger, and the streets and canals, virtually empty. She arrived at the palazzo and climbed the stairwell-gullet and only then understood her husband's refusal to meet her at the airport: usually so smart, he was dishevelled now, would barely meet her eye, and was very thin, as though practically having gone without food in their six months apart, the writer was quick to ask about the state he was in, his only reply being to look away and answer with a terse 'Nothing, it's nothing, how was your flight?' She, to avoid adding confusion, decided not to tell him about the man who had sat next to her, 'Fine, the flight was fine, just a bit of turbulence when we were taking off. By the way, what's going on in the city? It's like a desert,' a comment he did not react to either; he did not even bat an eyelid when she took the snowglobe out of the bag and handed it to him, a miniature that only a few months before he would have marvelled at, but that he now simply put back in the bag, before disappearing into the bedroom. It was then that, following behind him, she entered that room – he had immediately got under the covers – and saw the large vinyl sphere for the first time. It stood on the bedside table in the lamplight, on an improvised pedestal made of small objects that, from the makeshift look of their assembly, looked to her like they must have been picked up in the street, or out of a rubbish bin somewhere. She went over to the sphere, its blackness giving off a wet sort of heat; she reached out to touch it, but drew her hand back at the last moment. Nor did she dare ask any questions. Only on the third day, days that unfolded virtually without a word from either of them – him spending more and more time in the bedroom, lying down beside the vinyl sphere – and her, wanting to feed him up, spending the whole time cooking meals of every kind, from the very plain to the exotic, did he open his mouth to say: 'You don't only make rice with beef now,' to which she said, 'I start making the recipes from the old days and they come out just like that, it's as though I've been cooking them my whole life.'

The next morning, she was making breakfast when he appeared in the kitchen – straight out of bed – and sat down to watch how she handled the herbs and spices, and with no preamble began to speak: 'After you left, a few weeks passed, and I started to feel like something wasn't right. A tickling sensation came over me, particularly at night, at first it was only in my legs and arms, but it soon spread to my whole body, and then, when I got into bed and closed my eyes, it turned into a sort of mental tickle, my thoughts quivered and shook, they shuttled around constantly, like somebody swapping the book you're read-ing every few milliseconds; nothing made any sense. I sometimes found myself sitting there for whole minutes at a time watching a bird peck at things on the windowsill, or the blue flame on the kitchen stove. I got up in the night one time and went and sat on the living-room sofa; in the darkness, everything looked grey, but a sort of en-riched grey, with every granule of dark ever so slightly different from the one next to it, and that gave me some relief because it made my nervousness subside – even Alexa's blue ring, the slow pulsing of which broke up the darkness, now felt pacifying. But around that same time I started hearing footsteps in the apartment above, foot-steps that seem to belong to a single person, and that went back and forth along the hall, into the kitchen and then to the living room or balcony; thinking there was no one living there, it felt really disconcerting, but I still couldn't resist getting up in the night sometimes and following those footsteps around, tracing the same path around our apartment, mirroring them from one end of this place to the other, until they would stop and I, down here, would also go back to bed. This went on for more than a month. I was initially intrigued at the different paths this person would take, I found it entertaining, a simple game, but after another month I started getting tired of it – following the footsteps no longer made me feel anything. And again, I started to get up every night and, sitting half-naked on the sofa, to think about you, so far away then that I felt nothing, any union between you and me seemed to be over, and, rather than this causing me any pain, I felt like it just didn't matter. Days when any routine, even eating and washing, started to feel like an inconvenience, to say nothing of leaving the apartment, which I found myself doing less and less, and when I did, all I found was that my separation from the world was growing greater all the time, and I then thought of the city as a book in which the words were being pushed further and further apart, and the white spaces growing so much that when you get to the next word you can't remember anything about the previous one, and the overall meaning disappears, as though it's been erased, to the point where, to try and get it back, I came up with the idea of going to the places you and I had gone when we were here together. One day I put my jacket on directly over my house clothes, did the buttons all the way up and set off along the same routes we'd walked together. To begin with, I was doing this at no particular time of the day, but after a few weeks I started remembering the hours when you and I had gone on this or that particular walk, and tried to bring them to life, although, truth be told, this had no effect whatsoever. I went by the place where we found the white blouse in the snow that day with its beating heart, and I imagined you'd be wearing it in Montevideo – I see you still are – and I bought the same black-and-white postcard of Venice, the one with the bird's-eye view of the city that makes it look like a mountain range, and I spent a lot of time looking at this postcard trying to find something, though I had no idea what, like when you feel drawn to some odious person and can't understand why you keep on looking at them, I became so obsessed with that postcard of Venice as a mountain range that I came to detest it. And I took the same gondola we took together and went along the same canals, finally coming out at the place where the Biennale is held, those leafy gardens you and I never managed to visit, and I was amazed to find all the different country pavilions had been taken over by people of just about every nationality, a sight to behold, with tents and clotheslines hung from the outsides of the buildings, and the smell of all kinds of cooking I didn't recognize, and tables and chairs scattered throughout the gardens of the complex, and I couldn't understand any of this, and I left, and I even walked to certain neighbourhoods where you and I hadn't been, slices of the world so quiet they seemed like pictures of themselves, and I tried to get into St Mark's Square but couldn't get anywhere near it, some days before that, the total of absence of smell and sound that had previously been only inside and in the immediate vicinity of the square, had begun to move outwards towards the nearby canals, and later into every single canal in the city, pockets of absence and emptiness that came and went, popping up now in different places around the city, deferred signals of something to come, and that did come, my God did it come, every day I saw more and more blind people, an unequivocal sign that they had passed through one of those pockets in which the world had been hollowed out, and if they weren't yet blind they were on the way to becoming so, because they kept bumping into one another, people suddenly falling into canals, inexplicable drownings, gondolas and boats crashing into one another for no apparent reason, and I then felt certain that the only way to avoid being affected by that blindness myself, or by that absence of sounds and smells, was to shut myself up here in the palazzo, a voluntary confinement that seemed like the most sensible solution, so I shut all the windows and from then on the light coming in through them was just about the only out-side light I got. I spent at least a month walking these rooms, ordering takeaway once a week from the big fast-food chains, the only ones that carried on functioning normally because, as I later found out, they had a legion of men and women of all ages and nationalities waiting to take the place of the next worker to lose their sight – these delivery people would come by bicycle and leave the bags at the door. I started hearing the footsteps upstairs again, and every night, when they stopped, and when I had fin-ished copying them down here, I would come and sit on the sofa again, precisely where you're sitting right now, and I'd see the same things you're seeing: the same table with the veins that look like sea water, the same high win-dow, the same domes of St Mark's, the same brushstrokes on the frescoes, the rug which, I don't know whether it is Persian or not, but looks like it is, I saw everything you're seeing right now, but one night I saw something else – don't be too alarmed, but – one time, in the early hours, the men in the blue jumpsuits came back, the men from the dream, there they were, real as anything, carrying those same big cardboard boxes in their arms. It was they who confirmed to me that these boxes were empty, and that they had been wanting to fill them up for years, fill them up with something they didn't initially specify. They said they had always been looking for proof of a strange infection that had broken out in Venice's baptismal fonts many years before, which had killed all the affected babies but one, but that in reality the search for this illness was only a cover, or, more than a cover, a symptom of something far greater, namely the lack of love, because this was what they were really looking to do, to bring love back into the world. The lack, they said, had manifested more than 80 years before with the contamination of the holy water in the city's baptismal fonts. And, they said, the love was something that you and I could now bring back in, they told me, because they were certain that it's within our power, you and I, to restore the love, to make it a moving force in the world once more, and certain, too, that we hadn't come to this property by accident, and they therefore asked me that we stay very attentive to anything, any sign that might hold this key, and said they'd come back soon to see if we'd found anything that could be of use to them, and that they'd leave the boxes here so that if I did find something, I could fill them, they said they'd be sure to come and pick them up, so said the youngest of the men, who seemed to speak for all of them, and he then paused and I glanced over at the window, it was dawn, the sun lighting up the domes of St Mark's, still snow-covered though it was just about spring by now, the wings of the lion on its plinth, slightly curved at the tips, shone like those of an aeroplane up above the clouds, and when I turned back to the door, the men had disappeared, leaving the boxes by the door, and I felt so utterly afraid that I threw the boxes out the window, straight into the canal, just as I'd done with the boxes we found the morning you left for Montevideo, and I watched as they floated

off down the canal, within moments the cardboard started to liquefy like ice in the sun, until they eventually
melted into the water, and I heard the same footsteps as
ever upstairs and I started following them, they went to
the bathroom, after a minute of going nowhere, I heard a
flush, and I flushed the toilet down here too, and together
we went back to the bedroom, where I got into bed but
without falling asleep, I lay very still but at the same time
was feeling very uneasy, like a mouse in the snow, trying
to find the heart of an idea that would help me to process
all that I'd seen and heard. It would have been midday the
next day when, barely having slept, and still in bed, I remembered the thing I'd told you about car crashes and
needing to turn towards the place the accident was taking
place, towards the crash itself, because every collision is a
moving event, and when you get there the accident will
have moved on to a different place, and this thought
brought with it a hunch, an intuition: what I needed to do
was go out and walk the streets, but first I picked up the
black-and-white postcard of the city, the one that made it
look like a mountain range, and on an impulse I set fire to
it, I took it to the kitchen stove and watched the slow tide
of fire rising up through the streets, churches and canals,
witnessed this image of the city disappearing forever before my eyes; it's rare to see something that's at the same
time ceasing to be seen. And it was then that I knew, without a shadow of a doubt, that what I needed to do was go
out and start walking the streets, to try to find a collision,
though what collision I had no idea, find the thing that the
men in the dream said could restore love to the world. I
took my first shower in I don't know how many days, put
on my usual clothes and left the palazzo resolved not to
come back until I found what I was looking for. In the
streets, and far more frequently than in earlier months,

the only people I saw looked like they were strolling aimlessly, heading nowhere in particular, women and men who, wrapped up in their own thoughts, were counting their own footsteps or bumping into one another, falling over and cracking open their heads. I passed the taxidermy shop, the leopard that had hypnotized me six months earlier was now totally dissected in the window display, it was as though its eyes, which seemed very much alive, were taking on the vision that the humans were losing moment by moment, and I carried on and there was not a single boat or gondola on the canals, and apart from four or five franchises of large food corporations I found all the shops shut, and so, not being able to travel by water, I continued all the way by foot, I'd never realized how long it takes to get anywhere in this city without the shortcuts provided by the canals, and I pushed on like somebody typing away at a never-ending text and again came out at the grounds of the Biennale, where the mix of cultures I had seen a few days earlier had increased, lots of food delivery bicycles were parked there, there was a row of them stretching as far as the eye could see, I supposed that more than one of these men and women had come and delivered food to me over the weeks, and all the pavilions were full of people, all except the Austria pavilion, which stood deserted, as though some kind of epidemic were being incubated inside it, in its very walls. I spent a short while in the communal gardens, not finding the collision, the accident I was looking for there either, and I went away again and continued on and later, tired of meandering the city so long, I saw a shop in the distance with its shutters up, the first open shop I'd seen all day, and my feet led me directly there as though it were a lighthouse; only when I was a little way off did I realize it was the record shop you and I went to together. I pushed on the door, which swung open with barely any resistance; there was nobody inside. I stood there for a few seconds before beginning forward between the crates, under the same yellowish light as in our visit months before. Someone suddenly drew a curtain behind the counter: it was the man who had taken me down to the recording studio in the basement that time, he was wearing the same blue suit and, the moment he saw me, he said, 'Come through, we've been expecting you,' and I, petrified, stood stock still, could neither move nor speak, and seeing me just standing there, again he said, 'Come through, come through, we've been expecting you,' but since I did nothing, he went on: 'As you wish, I'll bring it out myself,' and he went away for a couple of minutes and came back carrying a vinyl sphere, which he put in a plastic bag with the utmost care, saying 'it's the one that you, gripping my hand, recorded six months ago, consider it a gift,' and he handed me the plastic bag, it was tremendously heavy, I could barely lift it, and there was a warmth coming from it, a wet heat, like my body heat – a blind person would have thought it a protuberance that had grown on my very skin – and, turning on my heels, I left the shop, I set off walking again, finding myself able to now, now that I had the objective of coming back here, but I needed to stop every few metres to rest, the weight of the bag was almost too much for me, and I didn't get back until very late that night, the bag and its contents safe and sound, and I immediately took it out and put it on the bedside table, along with some other objects, bits and pieces I'd picked up during all my walks, and in the days until you've come back, I've been lying next to it, observing it, receiving its warmth, at first as though it were yours, the warmth of you that I was missing, but then the sphere started to express itself and its heat came to be what I was looking for, this sphere is a star, wholly and entirely a star, the nucleus of love, which is what makes it expand and contract without ever exhausting it, a love that pulses and not only fills my days and nights but also my dreams; I don't know what I would do without it. I then thought I understood that this was what the men in the dream were looking for, this vinyl sphere, the sphere that contains everything and knows everything about love, the sphere that can bring back universal love. Since then, watching over it to the best of my knowledge and ability, I've been waiting for you.'

He falls quiet; his breakfast plate untouched on the table. She has just finished hers and, not knowing what to say, she looks over at the windows in the back room; lightning flickers on the horizon, a storm is approaching, the first of the early summer storms. Turning to her husband again, she says: 'How about we take your sphere apart and listen to those vinyls?' 'No,' he says, 'a lifetime wouldn't be enough to listen to them all, the man in the shop was very clear about that.' 'That makes no sense,' she says. 'Yes, it does,' he says, 'it makes all the sense in the world,' and he immediately gets up and goes back to bed, lies down, closes his eyes but does not sleep, feels the heat of the sphere and feels the movements of his wife, who has gone into the next room, a study in which she has just for the first time taken a portable typewriter out of a metal case. After a few minutes he will hear her starting to type, a sound that will go on throughout the morning and into the afternoon and evening, and all night, and through the succeeding mornings, afternoons, evenings and nights too, to constant thunder and lightning, and several days pass with the writer typing non-stop, many broken nails, and the storm has settled over the city, a relentless battery, and the small snowglobe of Venice, placed on the desk by her, has bobbed this way and that to the striking of the keys and is now at the edge, about to fall to the parquet floor, one more letter would be enough to make the snow rise up again and a minuscule snowflake fall on St Mark's Square and all of Venice go tumbling down, but no, it will not be a keystrike that gives the final push but rather the sound of the doorbell, which rings, it rings this very instant, a doorbell so loud that it makes the writer start, and the same with her husband in bed, a doorbell so seismic that the globe teeters and, now, indeed, begins its vertical, clean, unimpeded dive, and smashes on the floor, buildings and canals in pieces, imitation snow everywhere, glass ceiling shattered, and she in the study and he in the bedroom, both still paralyzed by the doorbell, at a loss, it is the first time this doorbell has rung, they can't bring themselves to react, each of them in their separate places can't bring themselves to react but they know that were they together, their paralysis would be just the same. After a few minutes they get up, go towards the door, somebody has slipped a piece of paper under it, she crouches down, there is some handwriting, she reads it out:

'Good morning. I'm your upstairs neighbour. I only wanted to introduce myself and say hello, I'll stop by another time. The ambassador.'

IV.

Why are we afraid of the dark if it is an absence. (*Subtraction love*)

Your life and mine are infinite, they cover entire millennia. The rest of humanity does not understand this timescale.
   – she says.
Our mission is to ascertain the epochs of terrestrial love.
   – he says.

Love, like rocks, can be igneous, metamorphic or sedimentary, and because of this the processes that cause our feelings to mutate correspond to these three rock formations: crystallization, metamorphism and sedimentation. Beyond these geological limits, all love is imaginary. (*Rock love*)

Life assigns us all a task that is beyond us, something that even over the course of various lifetimes we would not be able to achieve.
   – he says.
I often remember the street cleaners, the way they used to bring the streets back to life.
   – she says.

The family is, by definition, a secret society. And as if this were not enough, it sometimes in turn hides a secret, an ancient episode latent in the darkness of generational time, and then this secret society becomes doubly secret. The concentric ring of secretiveness triples when the crime still exists. The secret is then handled like an ember of uranium passed from one hand to the next until the fingerprints of every family member are erased, making them all equal in their love of this thing that may never be named without its corresponding judgement and sentence; it then manifests when the person who has named it is expelled from the tribe. (*Concentric love*)

Love is a fantasy.
   – she says.
But one of precision.
   – he says.

Technology, in all its forms but especially since the appearance of electronics and later of social networks, has grown exponentially. Our perception of our environment, however, does not grow exponentially but always at the same rate, a linear rate. These two phenomena being so out of step indicates, in the first place, that for many years now technological advances have been moving beyond our apprehension of our environment – increasingly less immediate and more vast – and secondly that a day will come when technology's exponential growth will be an almost vertical line, and at this point we won't even be able to detect what is around us. By then there will be no human perception capable of attending to such a change; the technological milieu will simply escape us. But this also indicates that love – something that appears suddenly and instantly in the human, and which therefore does grow exponentially – will be the only thing capable of accompanying technology in its flight to infinity. Love will then be the solitary witness, the only thing to see what is happening. It is not the 'Internet of Things' that will save us from individual solitude, but the love of things. It could even be that, through the elementary laws of viral contagion, love will become technology and, vice versa, technology will acquire a halo of the love drive, only possible until now in the spines covering the thighs of fairies and in the solitary eyes of the cyclopes. (*Exponential love*)

Here the dead get cold and hungry sometimes.
– he says.
No. The only organic function the dead continue to perform is sex. Everything else they erase.
– she says.

Mistakes do not exist in physical processes. We cannot speak of mistakes in the formation of a star, in the expansion of electromagnetic waves or in the disintegration of an atomic nucleus. Nor are there any such things as pathologies in the physics of either the macrocosm or the microcosm, and any supposed anomaly in nature will sooner or later find its place in a coherent theory. This is not the case in biology, where we sometimes see talk of cellular malformations, people with mental disabilities, defective genes, etc. That which we call a 'mistake' is an arbitrary moment of adjectivizing, the result of a cultural convention disguised as necessity, or, ultimately, a kind of defective love felt by a civilization towards itself. (*Pathology love*)

In what moment did we invent this language which is ours and ours alone.

– she says.

The day we understood the uselessness of the lines on our palms, and then the lines on the soles of our feet – muddled but already completely delineated – rose up into our mouths and stayed there.

– he says.

When children find out that the Father Christmas isn't real, or that his magic was mere trickery, it's usual for them to feel disappointment. The child learns something in this moment that she or he will never forget: all mystery is a by-product of language, whether written, visual or gestural, and what lies behind this body of signs is always something banal or uninteresting. Or indeed: magic tricks and their associated mysteries are in themselves language. The enigma of the Rosetta Stone – which once it has been decoded tells us little of any consequence – is not in the stone itself but rather in the journey, the fable, that must be undertaken to achieve its deciphering. Nor does the mystery of CCTV cameras reside in what we see on their screens, which as often as not are banal moments; the camera itself creates the mystery. For this reason, even the most innocent, everyday image seen through these screens – a flower opening at dawn, two friends shaking hands, a woman throwing a rubbish bag in a dustbin, the birth of a foal – as if by magic becomes a shady, sordid, dubious event. There is only one exception to this rule: the beloved person is the only language that can never be decoded, the only site in the world where reality and magic truly coincide. (*Code love*)

With you, I have learned that kissing is the only human activity in which air is expelled at the same time as it is taken from the other person.

   – he says.

There is no greater physical mystery than the union of two mouths.

   – she says.

The only possible way to enter yourself is to go to the nearest pond – a swimming pool would also serve – position yourself on the edge and, when there is no wind to distort it, throw yourself into your own reflection. But what happens then is that, just before you hit the water, the air generated by your onrushing body will distort your reflection, which will then be different to the one you were looking at moments earlier, making this method imperfect. The opposite variant is suicide: once one has thrown oneself over the cliff edge, one falls but also ascends, feels oneself rising to meet one's reflection, sublimated above, a reflection one never ultimately meets. Someone exactly like us shouts to us from many places, all of them inaccessible. (*Narcissus love*)

I think that some of the things we are seeing at the moment were there before the Great Blackout.

   – he says.

The past is the only part of life that remains. The past is holy. Every person is a sacred shape, a walking altar.

   – she says.

Global Love is nothing but a fantastical extrapolation

based on things that do exist, like the Global Market, Global Warming, the Global Network, Global Migration, etc. (*Global Love*)

The valley that goes upwards from the house and tails off among the snowy mountains resembles the jaws of a snake, which, to take in their prey, open as wide as they can before dislocating completely.
– he says.
My sex has been doing the same for you, for a thousand years. I see no problem with it.
– she says.

The difference between reading and studying is that the person who studies also underlines things. Underlining is completely different from reading, it is closer to intervening in or rewriting what has been given to us, but without betraying the originality of what is given. Love can only be conceived on the basis of this underlining: to love is to rewrite the other. The windblown sand also hits the coasts and rewrites in dust that which in the cities was taken as settled. (*Underlined love*)

A man once told me that the only way to create duplicates is to burn portraits and photographs of the things.
– she says.
The Earth's core itself and the stars are nothing but perpetual bonfires.
– he says.

Thelonious Monk: 'It's always night, or we wouldn't need light.' (*Night love*)

In the place you go in your dreams, you give names to the things on that other side, while everything you have left behind in waking life stops growing for want of light.
    – she says.
Even the alarm clock stops.
    – he says.

Errors, when they extend throughout society, are not only convenient but useful for keeping the peace, because they are unassailable. When an error is configured as part of a system, it gives rise to an ideology, which is the definition of that which does not question itself. If we replaced 'error' with 'love' here, we would get the same result. (*Error love*)

A number of months ago – if we can talk in terms of time – on my way to seeing the tadpoles in the river, just before I got to that last remnant of steel that we always find amusing and terrifying in equal measure, I met a man who looked at me and walked as though he were on a cloud, or as though transported on the backs of a legion of beetles. He seemed to have a body on the other side already.
    – he says.
On the other side, all languages are dead languages. Let that man go and not come back.
    – she says.

In the old documentary movies, originally in black and white and later in colour, faces, clothes, vehicles and buildings were usually the main attention of the set designers' focus, along with more striking areas of woodland, but the artisans responsible for these brushstrokes always left something in the still unpainted, a stretch of black and white now become a distant plane of reality, a genuine Deep Time that, until this moment, had presented itself as homogenous Historical Time. When you look at one of these movies you feel that, paradoxically, it is this part of the landscape left in black and white that supplies the rule of verisimilitude to the new scene in colour. Similarly, love does not admit any colouring-in after the fact. Love is not even in black and white, it is far beyond such tonal differences; it is either purely black or it is nothing at all. Love is an object to which the same thing happens as to the entrails inside our bodies, viscera that only function correctly if the surgeon's knife has never sought them out, if they have never been touched by the light – kept in absolute darkness. (*Viscera love*)

My love, the pebbles in the river sometimes walk backwards though there is no crab inside them. A firefly shines in the darkness more intensely than any photon of sunlight. In everything there is always the shadow of another thing that is either equal to or greater than it.
– he says.
I told you, all the snow was already in the ocean. Every person is a walking altar. The temperature that makes my nipples dilate is you, illusion of straightness in this world full of curves.
– she says.

The solution to a problem necessarily grows out of the seed of that problem – a solution that will later be a problem, and so on, successively. This is not open to question. (*Non-homeopathic love*)

We make up a binomial that casts a spell on the soul of things.
– he says.
In the depths of the night, the objects around us – space itself, even – turn luminescent. There is no greater sorcery than this.
– she says.

That we are in a time dominated by magical thinking is demonstrated by the incontestable fact that people increasingly make less of a distinction between metaphor and reality; the metaphor is assumed to be a truth, in its strict literalness. It is not that metaphors aren't true, and far less that they aren't real – they are at least as real as a theory – but rather that they have a different nature, the nature of analogies, figures that, while they relate to what we tend to call 'reality', bring something else into being: the maturity of an intellect that sees relations between things without confusing them as one and the same. In every period marked by magical thinking, it is more common than ever for love – the only thing that is not a metaphor for something else, the only thing that is raw material for the world, the only thing that, were it to become visible, would make us tremble in pure terror – to be subject to the fantasy-making of poems and made-for-TV films, of politics and markets. But there is more: if we consider it to be true (which it is) that only humans understand

what a 'representation of reality' is (dogs do not distinguish between the rules governing a tree and a photo of a
tree, they see both as occupying the same plane of reality),
then only humans comprehend what a metaphor is,
precisely the opposite as happens in periods marked by
magical thinking, periods that therefore come to belong
to animals. But there is even something else: if animals
do not distinguish between the tree and the photo of the
tree, it is only humans that detect what we can call a 'lag'
in the perception of the two things, a difference, a kind
of vertigo similar to that which exists between the magic
number and its corresponding trick, between the character and the real-life actor. Hellenic physics knew this, and
Newton did too, but it was not until Einstein's arrival that
cause and effect could be shown as not instantaneous,
that between the effect and its cause there must always
be an intermediate time of interaction, a 'lag', and that no
line connecting whichever events can be faster than light.
That human – only human – 'lag' enabling us to distinguish reality and metaphor, tree and photo of tree, is also
a maximum line of light that submerges magical thinking
in a cheap trick. Well, this very vertigo produced by the
lag is love; but the love of the real. (*Lag love*)

In these months away, I've seen people love one another
who no longer love themselves, I've seen the bolus of the
sun wane in a dirty half-light, I've gone through days subject to the systematic time of earthly Botox, and heavenly
vessels announcing their own coming but then instead
the arrival of pagans converted to religions that venerate
gold and animals, and I have also walked lonely streets
when the people were all asleep, which was to cross a desert peopled with dreams. There were times when, inside

one of these dreams of people I didn't know, you would suddenly appear.

    – he says.

In your absence, I have not stopped thinking about you. At no moment has the image of you left me. You are the totality of all that I know.

    – she says.

Taste is not a question of aesthetics, nor far less a pose, but rather a survival mechanism, principally to establish, by their bitterness, which foodstuffs might be poisonous. Love is taste in its most powerful guise. (*Taste love*)

When we shut ourselves in the bedroom during the day and lower the blinds until not a single chink of light can enter, we create an artificial darkness so dark that our bodies emit light by themselves.

    – she says.

That is when all the information in the world finds itself contained in the two of us. We emit it with no shame.

    – he says.

Contrary to popular belief, it is in our day-to-day activities that we wear a disguise, a mask; in fact, it is in supposed transvestism that our most secret, primordial self emerges, the thing we really want to be but cannot. At a masked ball, then, the only person in disguise is the one not wearing a costume. It has become common to say that fictions are invented in order to live other lives, to experience everything we are not and never will be, but nothing could be further from the truth. It is impossible to kill somebody in a novel or to be Attila the Hun in a movie without previously having felt the desire to kill or to be the tyrant Attila the Hun was. Fiction does not hide things; on the contrary, it allows them to emerge as they truly are. Love is the only exception: you take off the mask and always find another, which is the same, its identity that of the infinite disclosure of the identical. So it goes, and every time a couple argues it ends in a draw – or they aren't a couple. (*Mask love*)

To love someone is to admit that there is also something in them that frightens you.
   – she says.
And yet, with you I don't tremble.
   – he says.

Sand, because it is used in all kinds of construction work, is one of the most highly prized goods on the planet. But the sand from beaches cannot be used in construction work. The reason for this anomaly is of a physical order: grains of sand from beaches are rounded, they do not have corners, looked at under a magnifying glass they are like pebbles from a river, meaning that when put together with cement dust there is almost no friction between the two materials, they do not bind together, there is no emulsion; like tears, the grains of sand fall to the bottom of the mixture. Quarry sand is required for cement, sand that has recently been crushed and ground and therefore has rough edges, with corners and jutting protrusions that give these grains the resistance to stop them from falling. What we have just said, anybody could convert into a metaphor for a multitude of different things. One could look no further than conflicts between governmental powers (cement) and the citizenry (grains of sand). Or than love. It's so easy, it isn't even worth doing. (*Sand love*)

This brilliance of ours lasts for an instant and then disappears, never to return. We are that which is seen only once, nor do we even have a name.
   – he says.
But what becomes of the flakes of your skin when I lick you, and of the drops of urine on my sex when you bury your face down there and inhabit that place until I come apart, what becomes of all this if they are things that will constitute our legacy down the ages, our echo on the Earth.
   – she says.

Among the many strategies of conflict and war we find the one that consists of adopting the same tactics – exactly the same – as the enemy does. This was how the young chess player Judit Polgár beat the great Garry Kasparov in 2002; by imitating him. The chess genius would not only have buckled under the pressure of playing a woman in the highly macho environment of the sport at that time, but also learned there is nothing more punishing than competing with someone who replicates your tactics, your every move; defeating yourself is an impossibility. Some years ago, I had a dream of being chased, and as I fled I came to a house in the country and saw myself reflected in the front door, which was made of glass. When I got to the door and went to turn the handle, I realized that it wasn't my reflection there before me, but my pursuer, who, on the other side of the glass and disguised as me, was not only looking back at me but, as though from inside a mirror, copying my every gesture and expression. Logically (logic often bursts into dreams, although almost always pitted against us), immediately and without even having to try, the individual had me. With the immense quantity of personal data we save on the Cloud and in the thousands of hard drives scattered across the planet, it would be possible to reconstruct a very passable version of ourselves once we are dead. Selfies, voice messages, our body language in videos and a whole galaxy of archived details could be amalgamated and processed to put us back together again as convincing holograms of ourselves, meaning we can die confident in the embrace of this friendly, self-supplanting fire. But although the archetypes are constant, every constant also has its divergences, its variations, and love is no exception. The bonds that derive from love are resoundingly egotistical and reflective; the lovers' bodies are not really looking for the other or trying to learn what the other is like but rather looking for themselves in the other, who then becomes little but a tool, an instrument used to consummate said egoism. This is how, following the logic of the mirror, sooner or later the lovers destroy each other as they keep on looking only for themselves. (*Metadata love*)

The last high-voltage power line I saw was the one that used to be next to the canal. Its cables got tangled up in the wind; a knot was created while I stood there watching. The knot was the exact same shape as your sex. The wind was shaking the cables, the Great Blackout had just begun, and I stood looking at this knot of yours being bathed in rain and fire.

– he says.

171

I don't remember. But if you say it, I remember it.
– she says.

Blue is one of the colours that the brain takes the longest to identify; most four-year-olds have not yet conceptualized it. The reason for this is simply how rarely blue features in nature. The sea, seen as a whole, is blue, but there is nothing blue about a cup of seawater. The same goes for the sky: a portion of air held between our hands is never blue. The fact that when we look down on the Earth from a space station and are able to say that we live on a blue planet and not on a green, grey, pink or brown planet, indicates that, seen on a large scale, the Earth's enveloping shade – that is, the statistical median of all terrestrial colours, combined with the different atmospheric densities – gives a result that, when looked at on a small scale, becomes invisible, does not exist. This is a genuine 'apparition' of a colour as a result of the interaction of sunlight and the Earth's atmosphere. From which we can say that the branch of mathematics called statistics is the most fantastical and at the same time the most realistic version of reality. We see the same thing happening in love as well. When a large mass of people gather together – a football match, a concert, a political rally, a religious gathering – a union suddenly emerges between each and every one of those present, and certain special attachments that previously did not exist, which we could call 'statistical love', a kind of love that disappears when we remove a couple and consider them in isolation, for example in their domestic ambit, the affection and attachment here always being of a different and radical nature. A common error or misunderstanding often arises here on social networks. When Facebook tells us someone is our friend, it is referring to this statistical friendship, this statistical love, which does exist, but will turn out to be illusory if we take 'friend' to refer to the bond between two people. The love experienced by a couple, by definition, rejects every attempt to extend it to collective virtues and behaviours. A story: in a few months there is going to be a mass protest on the streets of a certain city, and a married couple, man and woman, are both in agreement with the cause, but the woman, more reserved than the man, does not feel comfortable in big crowds and decides not to go. Out of love for her husband, however, she volunteers to make some signs. She buys large pieces of fabric, and spends a month sewing them and painting the relevant slogans. And she does not know – there is no way for her to know – but when she gives them to her husband so that he and all the other protesters can walk into the city holding them aloft, the love between them as a couple, which has prompted her to stitch and paint and sew day and night, this love for which she has left her eyes and fingernails on every stitch of every placard and every letter of every banner, will in this exact moment be being destroyed by statistical love, the collective love in which her husband finds himself submerged, a human tide that will carry him away and from which – he also does not know – he will never return. (*Blue love*)

Years ago, when we first came to this house and you would get up in the morning and go out to get water from the spring by the path out the back, I would say to you I was going to sleep for a while longer, but that wasn't true. In your absence I would look at the wrinkles in the sheets, which still had the outline of your silhouette. When you got back, I'd hear you open the door, and your body would

173

disappear, the wrinkles would go back to being wrinkles and the sheet, a sheet.

– he says.

In the spring by the path, I also saw the water pouring out all kinds of different shapes. Now and only now do I realize that they were also wrinkles, your wrinkles.

– she says.

We are always dealing with this same doubt: what will the characters in movies think of us and our lives? It is the same with dreams: what would happen if somebody could see us from the inside of a dream? And it is the same with utopias, which for this reason are always impossible to realize: in essence, they are the same as cinema and dreams: from inside a utopia nobody can see us, nobody can perceive the lengths we go to as humans to bring utopias about. But neither can we see those who are inside them. If we think about love in these terms, we will see that it is the exact opposite of a utopia. Love either shows itself as reversible or it does not show itself at all, it is a vision of a round trip; naturally the object of love is able to see us from their side to the same extent as we can see them from ours. But – I wonder – what act of love-for-the-global-market, what kind of perfectly resolved utopia, prompts a young man to kill a tourist beside St Mark's Square in Venice so he can take his phone. (*Market utopia love*)

A kind of gluttony systematically leads my mouth to your sex.

– he says.

What is radical about the horizon is not that it can never be reached, but that it never stops moving.

174

– she says.

The window, from a construction point of view, is a source of light: the removal of filters. The window, from the point of view of the person inhabiting the house, is a way of looking out: the insertion of filters. Architecture is, in part, the attempt to solve this contradiction. There is a third function, not contemplated either by building techniques or by the inhabitant of the house: the gaze of the person who comes and, from the garden, uses the window to spy: the voyeur, the lover, the gossip, the removal of every filter in existence. This is a kind of love-violence. And it is here that architecture falls short in providing building solutions, where the inhabitant of the house, lacking any language to shelter in, expresses themselves like a newborn. (*Architectureless love*)

From the deepest part of the valley, the part we've never been to because it's the source of the river, and you and I hate everything that springs from the earth and neither asks for anything in exchange nor has any clear objective, there are vibrations with such a short wavelength that only I can feel them. They beat in my chest under my white blouse, like a second heart.
　　– she says.
It's the song, synchronized, of all those who have left us.
　　– he says.

In the same way that there are identity-less spaces – airports, motorways, shopping centres – that have been given the tag 'non-places' by sociology and urbanism, we can think about the existence of 'non-objects'. But unlike non-places, non-objects would not be identity-less, nor things so lacking in personality that they appear to not want to exist; on the contrary, we can imagine non-objects as objects that 'exist too much', as being so charged with meaning, so manifold in their adornments, forms and content, that all their meanings collide with one another in such a way that they are annulled, creating an object that is not only unique but also absolutely empty. Empty by excess, not by defect. Love is – par excellence – the supreme non-object. (*Non-object love*)

There is much talk about the lines on people's hands, about our destinies being delineated in them, but never about the lines on the soles of people's feet, which are the true makers of the path.

– he says.

A cap of mist has come and settled on the top of the mountain, you can't distinguish it from the snow. A nameless bird has made its way through this mist and this snow. I just saw it from the window; it looks like the first bird that came and landed on our windowsill after the Great Blackout. I think it's time to give this bird a name.

– she says.

From the Newtonian myth of action at a distance, to the no less mythological image of the butterfly fluttering its wings in India and unleashing a storm in New York, thus is our ancestral faith in magic. Or thinking that someone who died naturally has been murdered. Or a couple falling out of love, which is the murder of a third figure that is around us but we never see. (*Distance love*)

There is a movement towards the bone that is missing from my ribs, towards birds that have lost their way, towards a desert of lies with walls erected around them.
– he says.
In the Beginning there was also the darkness of a womb, and then a cry and tears at the contact with light. For this reason, tears and light are sisters.
– she says.

VENICE (4)

We left the couple holding a sheet of paper –
'Good morning. I'm your upstairs neighbour. I only wanted to introduce myself and say hello, I'll stop by another time. The ambassador.'
– a handwritten note that she has just read out. He says: 'Let's go up and introduce ourselves,' an idea that she, in her unease, roundly rejects. He questions this, and, again, she simply says no. They hear footsteps in the apartment above; someone walking to the kitchen, turning around and going back along the hall towards the front door. The couple go through into the living room. They look out at the city through the high windows, which are wide enough to give a view of the horizon, where further storms are moving in. There is almost nobody in the streets, a darkness like lichen or granite has spread over the buildings, very different to the white limestone from which Venice was built. They comment on the shape of the canals, some of which appear slightly bent towards

the east, others slightly shallower. They watch an ocean liner leaving the port, 'It'll probably be the last to do so,' he says. She quickly asks: 'How do you say "ocean liner" in Latin?' 'You can't. When Latin was invented, ocean liners hadn't been invented.' 'Now,' she says, 'a word will have to be invented for their absence.'

They go out that afternoon; it is the first time he has left the apartment in several weeks. They do not see a single gondola at any of the moorings, nor any vessels in the canals, which are empty of everything but water. The occasional passers-by feel their way along the walls, their memories of the streets to guide them. An elegantly dressed woman, walking with a stick bearing the words *I Love Venice* along the side, doubtless taken from an abandoned shop, walks along tapping the ground, making S shapes with the tip. He says: 'There's no difference now between these people and their shadows, which are also blind. They are one and the same.' Feeling suddenly frightened at these shadows, which in the couple's imagination become the actual living doubles of the bodies, they soon turn back. Come the night, over a supper of the few remaining provisions in the freezer, they try to arrive at an explanation for this sudden, unfounded fear of human shadows. After much consideration, they come to the idea that, in every moment, every aspect of our bodies is being passed between body and shadow, as though the two were interconnected vessels; if somebody loses a hand, the hand does not disappear, but instead gets passed to the person's shadow; if somebody has their gallbladder removed, it isn't lost, but instead gets passed to their shadow; if somebody is blinded, it is also the shadow that then receives the functioning eyes, and so it can always see. They find this improbable explanation sufficient to calm them for the rest of the night. She sits

178

down to rest while he, on an impulse, feels a desire to go and have a look around her studio, something he never usually does. On the writing desk, to the right of the typewriter, he sees a pile of typewritten sheets of paper, and skims through them; hundreds of short paragraphs concerning one single theme, love, pass before his eyes. Before leaving the room, he is still standing staring at the miniature version of Venice – which is lying on the floor in pieces that neither of them has bothered to sweep up – when the doorbell rings. They both jump. Each stands stock-still. After a minute, they go to the front door and find a note has been slipped through the gap; she picks it up, reads it out:

'Good evening. It's your upstairs neighbour again. I only wanted to introduce myself and say hello, I'll stop by another time. The ambassador.'

He again suggests they immediately go and see the man, knock and introduce themselves. She again refuses, and is even more set on this than before.

The next day, she says she wants to go to the old Biennale complex, to see what he told her about the pavilions of the world's leading nations being taken over by people of every class and country. He has no objections, though he does point out that, with no means of travelling by water, it will be a long walk, plus they will have to avoid the areas occupied by the vacuum-bubbles of smell and sound, which have grown to immense proportions. They make a plan to set out at dawn the next day, enough time to be back at the palazzo before nightfall. Provisioned with a couple of water bottles and energy snacks – dried fruits, dates and chocolate – they set out at 6 a.m. The day is cold; they set off walking separately, but soon find themselves holding hands. Without stopping, they see the whole of the sunrise, the warmth it provides barely seeming to touch their dawn-damp jackets. The only shadows are their own and those cast by the buildings they pass. The water, abnormally high in areas not usually liable to flooding, has partially covered many of the streets, which the couple are forced to skirt; only the churches are untouched, always being built, as is well-known, a few steps higher than street level. Before long they begin to hear rumbling noises inside the churches they pass, amplified by apses and domes. Finally, after a number of hours, they arrive at a street that ends in a canal, backtrack, take various diversions but find them all blocked by the soundless, smell-less bubbles, zones that announce themselves in intense bodily sensations as the couple approach. At the far end of an alleyway, they spot a gondola, moored to a building by a metal ring on the wall, water lapping at its sides. They go over. 'Even without any boats, these currents are never-ending,' he murmurs while she briskly unties the vessel; she has never operated a gondola before, but quickly works out how. They row along a series of connecting canals before arriving at a jetty, very near to the Biennale grounds, and she ties up the gondola, using several knots just in case; if it comes loose, she's aware they probably won't be able to get back. They walk no more than 100 metres before arriving at the gardens that mark the start of the grounds, and before they have gone very far along the tree-lined paths, are presented with a vista of the different buildings and the spaces that, having been nestled in gardens for over a century, have now been occupied by an extensive platform made up of pallets, wooden boards and pieces of rubbish. A multitude of people, adults and children alike, are out bathing in the faint sunshine as it filters between the deep, dark clouds of an incipient storm. The couple go on, leaving all this behind, and are soon afforded the sight of numerous pieces of art, previously housed inside the pavilions, which have been brought out and piled up to form what appears to be a play space for the children of the improvised commune. Other pieces of sculpture have been fitted out as makeshift huts, in which adults can be seen cooking on portable gas stoves. A brief walk takes them past the minimalist pavilion of the Nordic countries, which has been overlaid with bricks; only a small gap affords a glimpse inside, where a whole battalion of men and women of every ethnicity and colour are roasting what appears to be a deer. The neoclassical columns at the entrance to the oversized German pavilion have been painted different colours and used to fashion a frame for a low-doored wooden structure; they move closer and, before a woman's face comes out to meet them, see people standing around small fires, smoke escaping through an open chimney where the roof once was. Japan's see-through pavilion, Brazil's brutalist pavilion, Spain's fortified brick pavilion, Poland's ecclesiastical one, the United States' rationalist one, and on through the rest of the pavilions, nearly 30 in number; all – to greater or lesser degrees – have been transformed. Intending now to leave, they are making their way down the slight slope that leads to the exit, when a man stops them. With a curt nod, he asks what they are doing here, they don't know how to answer except with something that, although true, suddenly seems like a poor excuse: 'Pure curiosity.' The man tells them that everybody living here comes from countries that, when not locked in never-ending fratricidal wars, are starving, and that it would be best if the two of them left, that nothing in this camp could possibly be their concern, that they should go because, he says, 'The Great Blackout is coming and you need to be ready,' at which he returns to the people in his group, not giving the couple a chance to ask what he means by the Great Blackout, nor where such a thing might be due to take place. Going around the edge of the former central garden, they stop outside the Austria pavilion, the only one still with nobody inside it. A little further down, on the east side, the row of delivery bicycles he saw months before are now a mound of metal pieces and wheels piled up at the water's edge. They are about to leave the Biennale grounds when, in the middle of the central platform, standing on some boxes that serve as a pulpit, they see an elderly man, slim and silver-haired and wearing a blue double-breasted jacket with golden buttons and with a burgundy tie, using a megaphone to direct people as they transport works of art out of various pavilions. A crowd of men and women are depositing a multitude of sculptures, canvasses, video screens and photographs – photographs in particular – on the esplanade of the former gardens, which the large group then stands around admiring, but not for long. The man in the blue jacket with the golden buttons produces several canisters containing some kind of fuel derived from fossils, takes them over to the men and women but without giving any orders, without making any particular statement – perhaps in the knowledge that true power, the kind worthy of a monarch or a god, lies in making it known that one possesses the power and yet simply chooses not to exercise it, deferring it indefinitely, leaving it to exist only as a possibility or dream. Next, the men and women empty the canisters over the pile of objects, which become a flaming pyramid when someone from outside the circle enters in and hands a lit match to one of the children, who throws it on. Before stepping into the gondola again, the couple take a backwards glance. Hundreds of people stand in silence around a blaze that rivals the brightness of the sun.

And even, fleetingly, blocks it out.

After midnight, back at the palazzo once more and feeling unnerved by everything they have seen, he goes into the bedroom; lying down in the wet heat of the vinyl sphere, he closes his eyes and falls asleep. She goes into her studio, she wants only to sit at her desk, to rest, to think about everything they have seen. She has barely been back in this room since the snow globe broke – it remains in pieces on the floor. She goes over to it, looks down. The glass dome in smithereens, some of the shards so tiny they can barely be seen. The buildings, squares and canals, shattered and unrecognizable, look to her like the skeleton of an animal frozen beneath a patch of snow. She sits down at the desk, inserts a sheet of paper into the typewriter carriage, does not move her fingers but observes the amphitheatre of the typewriter keys, moments pass, she wants to type, but without knowing what else to write on the only subject of interest to her, love, she is unable to press a single key, the moments turn into minutes, so many that she falls asleep.

The sun comes up with the city under a layer of dark storm clouds, and the couple, him in the bed and her still asleep in the study chair, are jolted awake by the doorbell. It has rung several times, it has been held down insistently, so much so that they again do not dare to go and open it. The doorbell stops, minutes pass, and they eventually do go. A note underneath the door; she reads it out:

'Good morning. I don't know why you won't let me in, I only want to introduce myself, say hello, give you some final instructions. The ambassador.'

She, with unusual brusqueness, crumples up the piece of paper and throws it to the ground. She goes through into the bedroom, picks up the vinyl sphere from its pedestal, takes it into the living room and puts it down on the table in the middle; he does nothing to stop her, simply watches on. And then it is also her who opens the stereo cabinet and turns it on; there is a panel of lights on the amplifier, and this comes on, followed by the speakers, with a low electronic jolt. From beside it, Alexa, for the first time since being connected, also begins to emit a sound, a barely audible moan; her ring of blue light pulses in a way neither of them has seen before. The writer starts dexterously separating the records that make up the sphere. She takes the first one, which is no bigger than a coin and so hot that she has to toss it from hand to hand before she succeeds in placing it on the turntable. She drops the needle, turns the volume up, and a brief burst of noise comes from the speakers, a brief rumbling in which they think they can make out something like thunder. She takes the second record, which is a little larger than the previous one, gets it on the turntable; they listen to what appears to be the end of a thunderclap and then the beginning of what sounds like stones and other objects falling. She takes the third record, which is even hotter than the previous two, and when this one starts to play, it sounds as though the stones and other objects have hit the ground, and the sound of another thunderclap emerges, and then they listen to the next record, and the next one and the next, so many that they soon lose track, and these thunderclaps and sounds of cascading stones are followed by sounds of water overflowing, buildings collapsing, tree trunks dashing against one another, and so absorbed do the couple become in what they are listening to that they fail to notice the lashing thunder outside, and the canals as they begin to overflow, and the buildings collapsing and the tree trunks that form the foundations of the city being

184

irrevocably dragged out to sea, and they go on listening to the records, also failing to notice Alexa's eye blinking more and more, and when it begins to rain on one of the records, outside in the streets, the first drops of rain also begin to fall, and when on one of the records the lichen and mud down in the canals begin to cover what was once the city, these things also begins to cover the city outside, and when on one of the records it begins to snow, the first snowflakes also begin outside, and when on one record the first insects appear, the first insects also appear in what has by now become a valley outside, and when on one of the records a bird makes its first nest, a first bird makes its first nest outside, and when on one of the records St Mark's Basilica and the domes of the churches begin to form a mountain chain covered in snows that will come to be perpetual, the same begins outside, and when on one of the records the succession of putrid canals has already become the cleanest of rivers running between leafy trees, that same landscape has installed itself outside, and when wild animals arrive in the new-made forest on one of the records, the same is happening in the forest already springing up outside. It is only when they get to the final record, by which point the Protectress of Humanity's luminous ring has turned red, red like a newborn baby's bellybutton, that the writer and her husband hear a different sound, a confusion of breaths, like when you wake in the middle of the night and lie there listening to the breathing of the person beside you, and it joins together with yours forever more. Moments later, and for the first time, human voices emerge from the grooves, first a man's:

Where does it all come from, this whole landscape of wounds?

Followed by a woman's:

From bodies without passion, which are also landscape.

A bird – of a species so unknown that it has no name – flies through the sky, comes to the high window, flutters back and forth, lands on the windowsill and starts watching them. It watches them for a number of seconds, then takes off again and flies away into the trees.

They stand up. Two enigmas of flesh go out into the street, which is no longer a street. They feel a seismic swarming in the spirals of their throats, the tremor of the being who is inventing a language. They are about to say something. For the first time they call one another by name, Eve and Adam.

They continue this conversation, they converse day and night, months and years, so long that they will swap sexes and not know how. An exchange that will have no end.

Fitzcarraldo Editions
8-12 Creekside
London, SE8 3DX
United Kingdom

ISBN 978-1-80427-079-0

Design by Ray O'Meara
Typeset in Fitzcarraldo
Printed and bound by TJ Books

AC/E **PICCE**
ACCIÓN CULTURAL   Programa para la
ESPAÑOLA   Internacionalización de
                  la Cultura Española

The translation of this work has been supported
by Acción Cultural Española, AC/E.

Fitzcarraldo Editions